Thrown To The Wolves
By Maia Nunn

BAS,

HOPE THIS STORY SHOWS YOU THE WILDERNESS SIDE OF CANADA EVEN THOUGH ITS FICTION!

ENJOY,

M Nunn

Copyright © 2020 By Maia Nunn

All rights reserved. No portions of this book may be reproduced without written permission from the author.

First Edition: January, 2020

Cover Art by Wilde Marsh

Author:
Maia Nunn
For more information about upcoming books
or more about the author go to:
maianunn.wordpress.com

Dedication:

To Zoe,
My faithful Layrn through all of life's hardships and joys.

*"She had been sacrificed a princess of the people
but came back a Queen of herself."*

Sacrifice

"What-what do you mean?" her voice cracked; Myra's eyes widened as she stared into her father's gaze. His eyes held a fierceness Myra had never seen before. "Myra... Myra, I never meant for this to happen. I've done everything in my power to stop this, but the law demands it."

Myra shivered. "You mean to leave me here? Alone..." Her voice was quiet, still disbelieving.

This was her *birthday*! She was supposed to be going for a fun morning hunt with her father. She should be in the kingdom celebrating her transition to womanhood.

Instead, her father held a fur cloak in his hand, and a prayer that the Gods would take her swiftly to death. Her father gave a shuddering breath. "Myra, there's nothing I can do"

"No! Get away from me you monster!", she pulled away, flinching from his grasp. Her face set into a snarl,

"How dare you! You promised. You *promised*!", she screamed into his face.

"Myra, I didn't know you would have to be sacrificed. You know I would do everything in my power to keep you safe!". She stared at him. "You said I would never have to worry about the sacrifice. With mother gone there was no need to appease the Gods!". Her father held out the cloak, his guards behind him like judges over the proceedings. "You promised", Myra croaked. Snatching the cloak, she ran into the forest leaving her father standing in the clearing.

Layrn caught up to her soon after. The big pup bounded through the underbrush and nearly bowled her over in excitement.

"Layrn!", Myra cried, burying her head in his thick fur. "Oh

Layrn! What a good boy!" she cooed. He was big for his age. At only six months old he was already up to Myra's thigh. What he had in size he made up for in his playful, gentle demeanor. He was a gift from her eldest sister Liana. He wasn't a hunting hound, which was unusual for the royal family, but Liana had insisted, he was the one for Myra. She couldn't have agreed more. His lopsided ear and goofy grin would melt anyone's heart. Now, he was the only one Myra could rely on in these woods. They were alone. Myra hugged him more tightly.

Alone

Snow starts to come down in wet flakes, her fur coat has been her savior these past months, but she knows it won't last long. It had been made for special occasions, not survival in an unforgiving winter. Its seams are broken, the lining soiled with dirt and the fur begun to shed off in large clumps. Voices in her head claim she won't survive much longer. Myra ignores their warnings.

She has survived these woods for a few moons already, surely, she could survive a little longer. Couldn't she?
Her already thin figure now sticks out at uncomfortable angles. Her hips like weapons, her collar bones jut out in sharp relief. Her face is gaunt but still holds that spark of her old self.

Layrn barks and charges up to her, his doggy grin a sweet contrast to this unforgiving land. She laughs, lunging and chasing Layrn back to the shelter. Her exhaustion makes their playing short, while Layrn looks healthier than ever, Myra looks haggard and starved.

When they reach the shelter, both are out of breath and warm. It is then, Myra's ever tiring eyes blink slowly on the sputtering fire. Cursing, she trudges back into the forest, looking to the ground for more wood. Now, not only would they be hungry, they would also be cold!
Layrn bounds before her barking wildly at the forest, as if to ward off some invisible spirits. "Layrn! Quiet. We might still get

a grouse if we're quiet." He stops and starts to slink, looking excitedly for grouse, as she begins to collect twigs that lay on the ground.

When they return, it is starting to get dark. Layrn is happy. He had caught a tiny field mouse, and is now contentedly hungry, not grouchy hungry like Myra Or maybe that was from the cold that had permeated her fingers and toes.

She brushes tears off her eyes and moves the twigs into a better formation in the same fluid motion.
She works tirelessly away, spinning the twigs to create the friction required for a spark.
After cutting her hands several times with the sharp ends of the sticks, she throws them away in disgust. Her stomach gnaws at her. Making her double up in pain for a moment.

Layrn lays inside the shelter, a little grin on his face, his body unaware of the damp cold.
Myra laughs bitterly, tears starting to come in full throttle.
It had been months since her father had abandoned her in these woods, and not a soul had come to find her. None of her sisters, not even her friends in the stables. How had the king, as she had begun to call him, managed to convince all those people that she would not return and there wasn't something amiss? Then a frightening thought came to her, maybe every person she knew, both friends and siblings had known that this was to be her fate and so had only been close to her to keep her company until she was sacrificed. And when her father had come back from his hunting trip, what if the masses had cheered, because he had finally pacified their God?
If this was what God had done to her, she would never let a single prayer touch her lips again.

She shakes herself; it isn't the time for tears. She picks up the twigs again and this time a fire sparks to life, "Finally!" she cheers. Startling Layrn from a nap, he comes rushing out barking at nothing, and sways, his body still half asleep. He comes and lays beside her, his thick coat warm against her side.

She watches the fire, seeing figures in its fiery depths, and it reminds her of her middle sister Gwen. Gwen had loved fires, had loved to tell stories of the people stuck inside them, making up bizarre love stories and tragedies. It had always made Myra laugh. Now, as Myra watched the flames lick the air, she saw a glimpse of what her sister saw. "Oh Gwenny... dear Gwenny... Why did you have to love the fire so... Tell me again the story of Seraphina... Trapped beneath the flames by her father to isolate her forever from her lover, king of the water. Never to touch the flame of her beauty."

It is then that it strikes her, almost every story Gwen had told had been about a girl betrayed by someone or another and having to fight on her own to overcome her troubles.

Rarely did the stories have a prince that would save the princess in the tower, or when they did, something funnily tragic would happen to him. The Prince would be captured by the evil witch and become a llama or would fall in a hole-trap, stuck wailing like a child, until the princess had defeated her chains and saved him single-handedly. He would say something that would always make the girls go into hysterics, like "Oh noble princess!! I have been saved by your beauty and shall never underestimate the power of such a strong and handsome woman as yourself!" He would swoon and she would grab him by the arm and throw him onto the back of her noble steed and they would ride off into the sunset with the prince half on, half dragging behind, having missed his mark in the landing. Just the memory makes Myra smile, though it is but a ghost, hard to spot and gone in the split of a second.

And now it dawned on her again like a punch to her gut, how her other sisters had given her things to help her learn to survive in the forest.

Ariea, the youngest sister before Myra, had given her a bow and gave her lessons on how to fight with it. At the time Myra had been confused as to why she should need to know how to fight with a bow, but her sister had never answered the question, simply skirted around it.

Frieda had made sure Myra got riding lessons, and rode with her once each week, even though she was married and her time was so full of political meetings and courtly duties, that she barely had time to care for herself. Frieda had always said it was the best part of her day, to ride with her little sister, and forget that she was so burdened with courtly, womanly duties, and pretend for a while that she was a daring adventurer galloping for glory of unknown proportions. And, oh how they used to laugh. It had been a long time since she had heard Frieda laugh, even when she was still at court.

Liana (the eldest) had given her a dog, Layrn, whom she had said would protect her from bandits, usurpers, and courtly suitors. Myra had laughed at the last remark.
Her sister had several children of her own but had always invited Myra to join her in the kennels. It was an honor, for not even Liana's own children were able to go to her sacred kennels. "The dogs and the kennel", she had joked "are the only things that keep me sane. Without them, I would not have stayed as pleasant as I am now, and there's no way my children are allowed in there. It is my sanctuary from the children at times".
Myra's eyes became blurry with tears. *My sisters had prepared me for this day... had cared for me so I would be able to survive these forests.*
A sob escaped her. T*hey knew. They knew and had taken time out of their lives to show compassion and love to me, before I was sacrificed... The sneaky little buggers had secretly saved me from the sacrifice... Or longer to suffer.*
"Oh sisters! Don't abandon me now! I need you. Gwen - I need your stories to keep me sane, Ariea - I need your calm reassurance when I can't shoot an arrow straight. Frieda - I want to hear of your courtly duties and feel the horses' hooves galloping

over the countryside. And-... And Liana - I want to thank you for Layrn, without him, I would never have survived so long..."

Into the night her words were spoken, like a spell across the woods. Yet nothing happened. No knightly rider came galloping from the woods. Only crows cawed as they flew above the treetops travelling to their evening nesting tree.
Myra took a deep breath, the wood's silence filled her like water on a parched tongue.
It soothed her, and the rain that she heard trickling onto pine trees, was like a lullaby. The wind that had ravaged her during her hunt, now caressed her, blew her hair like a mother's stroking touch. And that was when she finally knew, not only would she survive in this harsh wilderness, but she would one day thrive.

That night she watched flames dance before her. Coyotes yipped in the distance. An owl hooted quietly somewhere in the tree canopy. Myra cannot sleep though because the betrayal eats away at her again. How could her father have let her live that long believing she would be part of the kingdom for her lifetime. He even had started suggesting possible suitors, as if he had no idea she had to leave. Had lied to her face for her entire life.
"How could you?!" she yelled out into the night, startling Layrn again. He jumped up from his sleep and galloped into the woods, barking. The sobs came unbidden. Layrn, after realizing there was no threat, came over to her; licking tears from her face. All her life she had been brought up to believe that she would be like her sisters; trained in the courtly ways and then married when she was of age. She knew her limitations, but she also knew how many possibilities she had, being fifth in line to the throne. It was as if a rug had been ripped from under her feet and now, she was falling, falling into an abyss that she had no idea the depth of. Everything that she had relied on; her sisters, her parents, who she was in the world, where she was destined to

go - was taken away. It would be only her and Layrn in this forest. But it was here her mind stopped. This was the abandoning wood was it not? She had not recognized it because her father had taken her here in such a roundabout way that she was confused and hadn't the faintest idea where she was. So there must be others, others abandoned by their parents in these woods... But what if, in their loneliness or their lack of knowledge, they had all perished? What if they had killed themselves, knowing they were no longer allowed in the kingdom? She had never heard much about the abandoned children, some parents took them to the forest as soon as they were born, others it appeared, much later.

Her tired body starts to sag, her eyelids drooping. She goes back to her bedroll, and stares into the fire, Layrn's warm body tucked in a ball on her toes. "First, I must survive, then I will go back... I will go back Layrn, and `I will make sure no other child has to endure this pain, no child need be abandoned."

Her father gallops into the forest, torches blazing, the entire kingdom behind him. He calls out "Myra! Myra!" in an increasingly hysterical voice. She can hear the drum of hoofbeats, can see the hunting dogs with their tongues lolling, "Myra!" Liana screams out.

Myra bolts upright, blinking into the darkness, a scream on her tongue. She stops, unsure now. It was a dream. Only a dream. But the urge to yell out into the forest, to call her sisters' names is strong. She waits, breath held, listening into the silence of the night. Nothing. *Oh! Of course not, you idiot! What did you expect? Everyone running back to get you, apologizing and sputtering excuses? Keep dreaming, Honey!* She crawls back under the covers. Liana's scream still rings loudly in her ears. Layrn comes up to her, she can't see him in the pitch-black darkness, but she can hear his shuffling, his quiet panting in her ear. She reaches for him, stroking his long thick fur. Layrn pants more happily as she strokes him "It's okay Layrn, it was only a dream... It was only a dream".

She awakens to chickadee song, and woodpeckers drumming away at the trees. Sunlight has just made it into the forest. When Layrn sees she's awake, he comes to her, his tail beating the air a mile a minute; a giant doggy grin covering his face.
At her feet lies a dead rabbit; its eyes bugged and its teeth a creepy, death grin. Layrn barks, bowing before her in play, his tail still wagging. She touches the rabbit's body; it's still warm, freshly killed. She grins. "It appears, Layrn, that we will be having rabbit stew this day!" He wags his tail even though he doesn't understand what she means.

She starts the fire again, her fingers numb. She pulls out the big rock that she uses for cooking and begins skinning and butchering the rabbit. This was one thing she had only watched a few times when she was but a little lass watching the cook skin the morning's kill. She hoped it wouldn't poison her, and then she laughed. It was funny that she should worry about dying from a poorly butchered rabbit, rather than hypothermia or an attack from a cougar.
The rabbit meat smelled mouth-wateringly delicious over the fire. She was intent on gathering whatever else she could so that she and Layrn would have their first full meal since they had been here. So, she went off in search for pinecones, lichen, and whatever else she could scrounge. Myra and Layrn returned, her arms were full of the bounty of the forest. Myra felt blessed to be so lucky to have a dead rabbit laid at her feet. As she got into sight of her camp, she saw smoke billowing up and Layrn's hackles rose. His deep growl penetrated the smoky air. She hears snuffling and then, low growling. "Oh dear…" she mumbles as three wolves appear out of the smoke, their mouths in snarls, her campsite in ruins. Layrn barks and puffs himself up to his full height, his tail erect and his body tense waiting to attack. "No Layrn!" Myra yelps in desperation. She looks at the wolves, their eyes golden and fiercely wild.

Layrn charges "NO!" Myra yells, dropping her bundle to tackle her dog. The wolves rush towards them. She only catches a bit of Layrn's fur before he's out of her, fighting with the wolves.

The wolves are massive, almost as big as a small pony. Myra screams in rage and fear, throwing pinecones, then rocks at the wolves. She tries not to hit Layrn, who takes the three wolves on at once. A fight ensues; the sounds sickening as yelps and snarls erupt from the masses of bodies. "Layrn stop!", she screams, rushing towards him. If she loses Layrn she won't ever make it out of these woods alive. She tackles one of the wolves who was about to make a leap at Layrn from behind. She knocks it over onto its side, growls like the wolves around her and screams in its face. "GET AWAY FROM MY DOG!" The wolf looks momentarily stunned by this new attacker. She seizes the moment to go after the other wolf, the largest of them, but her momentum isn't enough to knock it over. It snarls at her, clawing and biting as she tries to grab at it and scare it off with her yells. Tears stream down her face from the pain of the bites and from the unmistakable yelps from Layrn. As the wolf knocks her to the ground, her wrist smashes into a stone and she screams out in pain. Even as the pain shoots up her arm she gets an idea. She grabs the stone with her other arm, rolling onto her back to where the giant wolf is attacking. She whacks it solidly in the face with the stone. It yelps and pulls back. The others pause. Myra clambers unsteadily to her feet, gathering herself into a fighting stance. The wolf pulls back his lips from his teeth letting out a low, dangerous growl. "Well come after me then! You big coward!!" Her words sound hollow and scared.

She raises the rock in threat. The big wolf looks at her, twitches his ears then snorts loudly. The other wolves stop. Layrn lays on the ground, whimpering but still alive.

Myra's heart surges at his injuries, his ear looks like it has been ripped open and there is blood all over him. The wolves watch them, then the lead wolf seems to almost furrow his brows in confusion. He watches Myra for a moment longer then trots off toward the fire grabbing the last of the rabbit meat.

The other wolves follow him and they disappear into the forest without another glance. Myra stands there shocked at what just happened and comes out of her reverie with a skitter and a yelp from Layrn. She rushes to him, petting him gently and checking his wounds.

She hisses in pain as she sees his limp paw and tattered ear, the millions of scratches and bites along his body. "Oh, Layrn! My poor, poor dog! How can I fix this? This is all my fault! I should never have left that rabbit unattended.... I'm so sorry, Layrn". She goes to the campsite, her shelter is ruined; twigs, leaves, boughs and her bed roll are strewn about; ripped apart to find any morsel of food. The fire is sputtering out. She clears a spot, laying out her tattered bed roll as best she can with one hand. She rushes back to Layrn. She gingerly scoops him up. He yelps and squirms, but she hugs him close. "It's ok, it's ok, it's ok" she murmurs, walking over to the blanket and setting him down. She stokes the fire and rips her bed roll to make a bandage. She snaps the twigs once used in her shelter for a splint for Layrn. "Just our luck! I woke up this morning with a rabbit at my feet and I dare hope that by the end of this night I will not have-...not-...That you'll be ok-Layrn" she stutters. Her eyes fill with tears. "This is not the time Myra! You won't rest until you've got yourself a shelter made and something to fill your stomach..." But even as she tells herself this, she knows she won't let Layrn out of her sight again.

Myra watches Layrn for a long time. His eyes are closed in pain, his whimpers loud in the silent wood. Myra steels herself. *This is not the time for worry and sorrow, Myra.* She swallows back tears. Her wrist throbs as if its going to fall off. She closes her eyes, trying to take a deep breath. "It'll be ok, it'll be ok" she whispers over and over, shivering in the cold despite the fire. She does not sleep that night, tending as she can to Layrn's wounds.

She awakens to birds chirping cheerfully, singing songs of praise to the sun. She sits there confused for a moment as to why she is in the forest, and where her shelter has gone. Then it comes back to her like a tsunami and she sits up, her head whirling from the sudden movement. She looks to Layrn and a stifled sob escapes her. He is lying perfectly still, his good paw resting on her foot. She stops and watches for his breath. He is so silent her mind threatens to panic, but then she sees his breath shallow and quiet. She pushes out of her ripped sleeping bag and curls up next to him. She pets his side gently "Oh Layrn!" she croaks. He lifts his head slightly but is too weak to hold it and flops it back down again. She strokes his ears and they are like ice. "Layrn! You poor dog!" she scoops him up, putting him in her still warm bedroll. She rubs his good ear, his other just a shred.

Minutes pass like hours as Myra tries to figure out what to do for Layrn. The pain and exhaustion of the evening before must have knocked her out for a while because when she becomes conscious the sky is socked in by clouds. Light, fluffy snowflakes sparkle down in a last fighting ray from the sun.

Myra tries to focus her mind. It is a tumbling mess of half thoughts strewn about like a child's toys after the dog has run through them. She lifts her nose from beneath Layrn's fur, feeling the wet snowflakes and dog hair mix in her mouth. Spitting fur from her tongue she whispers gently in her beloved dog's tattered ear "Layrn? Are you awake?" His ear twitches as if tickled by her gentle breath. She smiles, tears in her eyes. She uncurls herself from around him and Layrn whines, his blood-soaked fur stiff and crystalized with ice particles.

Myra looks down at her aching wrist, it's swollen and purple. When she gingerly touches her fingertips, she can't feel anything, the tips are lightly blue and her mind panics. *oh my Gods! -I've got frostbite! My fingers are going to fall off!* The thoughts send her reeling and spots cover her eyes like a bright light has been blown out and now the imprint of it is tattooed on her eyes. *Stop! you need to get firewood; you need to keep Layrn alive and you need to calm down. Once you've done that then you can worry about your fingers falling off.* Slowly, delicately, she stands, her legs wobbling and her balance sending her lurching. She steadies herself with her good hand, palm against a tree.

Breathe Myra, you need to keep breathing. She staggers into the woods, already shivering in the snow. She manages to collect a handful of sticks within sight of Layrn.

After an hour or more goes by, a tiny wisp of a fire dances through the air, threatening to blow out if the snow gets any thicker. She grabs the bowl she carved herself about a moon ago and melts snow as best she can on the smoking, sputtering flames. *Clean his wounds, get food, stay alive.* Layrn is shivering even though he is wrapped in her blankets. "Don't worry, Layrn. I'm going to get you all fixed up. You'll see. Everything is going to be alright." She strokes his thick, polar bear-ish fur.

Layrn's shakes get worse. Myra tries to build up the tiny fire, but the twigs are wet, and the fire gets dangerously close to dying. Myra eventually just looks at Layrn. His body is shaking violently, and his eyes are closed shut. She scoops him up, he's too limp to even squeak in pain. And sets out into the forest, her tattered bedroll wrapped around her dog like a shield against his pain. The tiny fire spitting out as she goes out of sight of its tiny flames.

The Cure

She trudged through calf-deep snow, the wind blowing snow into her eyes. She was wandering. Searching for an answer, a cure, to fix Layrn. He lay quietly in her arms; she could barely carry his bulk any longer. Her arms screamed in furious pain. Better to feel this physical pain than the grief that burned a hole in her stomach.

Her knees gave way and she let herself fall, crashing into the snow. Tears crystalized on her eyelashes, threatening to seal them shut.

Layrn is so still and silent. *But, not dead!* she reminds herself. She is in a small clearing; the failing light making the snow glow a bone white. Trees stand like eye sockets in the haunted skull of the forest. She digs into the snow, packing its damp sides into walls. The sides will freeze tonight, and she hopes Layrn's little remaining body heat will reflect off the sides. She places his body in it, checking his wounds. Only one has gently started bleeding again but it isn't very much blood. She cradles his head looking into his golden eyes, they look glazed and distant, but despite his weak body his eyes show a little grin.

"I have to go get you some food Layrn. I... I'll have to leave you here. But I'll be right back! I promise. Don't leave me, Layrn. Hang on my boy. Just imagine! A hot, freshly killed rabbit or grouse roasting over the fire!" at the word grouse, Layrn's good ear perks slightly. "Yeah, you'd like that, wouldn't you?" She smiles sadly and kisses his muzzle. "I love you, Layrn", she whispers. Then, she is gone into the forest.

She returns a while after, two grouse dangling from their necks, over her shoulder. No triumphant grin paints her face; only grim determination. Layrn lies inside his little, half igloo. Snow has built up on his coat. She closes her eyes, "Please!" she whispers under her breath. When she touches his fur, it is warm. His tired eyes open blearily towards hers. Tears brim her eyes making her vision blur into confused shapes. She blinks, the liquid from her eyes spilling out onto her cheeks.

"Good boy! Oh, good boy! Look what I brought you Layrn. Two whole grouse! Just for you!" She can imagine that his tail would be wagging furiously if he had more strength. Instead he only gives a couple panting breathes of joy then sets his head down again. She drops the grouse at his toes and quickly snaps off low hanging branches of trees. But she knows everything is going to be too wet for this. She sighs angrily and throws the branches beside her, snatching up a grouse and producing a carved bone from her pocket. The bone is sharp enough to make a crude knife, so she butchers the bird. Plucking and shaving off feathers, then cutting its still-warm organs into little pieces, easy enough to swallow. Kneeling beside Layrn she wafts a piece under his nose. His nose twitches, but he's too tired to open his mouth. She opens it for him placing the chunk on his tongue and stroking his throat to make him swallow. If she can just get a little bit in him, it'll give him enough energy to keep him alive.
She works long after the dark has come and her fingers start to go numb, pushing little bits of meat into his mouth. Taking the occasional bite herself. Eventually she is too tired to continue and curls up beside Layrn in their little half igloo. Cold, but surviving.

Morning comes, chickadees call to each other in the pines. The air is crisp, and fog has settled at the tips of the trees. Myra stretches her painful limbs, her numb booted foot bumping into something. She looks up. A wolf stands at her feet, its feral eyes bearing into hers. Scrambling back, she slides into Layrn and he yelps. She freezes, wolves surround them in a circle.

"bloody bones!" She breathes.
The first wolf continues to stare at her, but not in a hungry way. She cautiously stands, trying to puff herself out as she had seen her father do with threatening subjects who thought they could push him around.
The wolf sits blinking up at her, and she realizes it's the one she had tackled when Layrn had been attacked. It was the leader wolf. "Go on! Get! Get outta here!" she yells her voice cracking in fear. The pack leaves, except for one. A small white wolf stands close to Myra. She swallows. The wolf walks towards Layrn her head bowed low and her stance
non-threatening. Myra waves her arms and yells at the wolf, but the wolf just skirts around her quietly and sniffs Layrn. It licks his tattered ear and he lifts his head weakly. Myra watches, stunned, as the wolf continues to each of Layrn's wounds and licks them delicately. When each wound was clean, the wolf looked into Myra's eyes pinning her in place for a moment. Then the wolf trotted off into the forest again; blending with the freshly fallen snow.

Time passes, Layrn sleeps quietly.
Myra watches the forest, the hair on her neck standing on end. The wolves surround them on all sides, quietly standing with their backs to Myra and Layrn.
A wolf watches from within the circle, it lays close to another and Myra guesses it's a younger one. It eyes the slowly rotting grouse by her feet.
Lifting the grouse by its frozen toes she makes her way to the wolf. "If you can't beat them you might as well join them." She muttered throwing the grouse at the wolf's feet. It leaps back expecting attack and grumbles, sending a ripple through the wolves.
Myra backs away slowly, the young pup watches her warily but snarls as another tries to steal the grouse at its feet. They grumble and snarl like that for a while until order is returned and they feast.

Myra stays hunched next to Layrn for a long time. She can't leave the grove, surrounded as she is by wolves. But if she stays without warmth for much longer her hands will go frostbitten... if they haven't already.
She stands again, putting the wolves on edge. Gathering the spindly twigs, she had thrown to the ground the day before, she snaps off more twigs, gathering enough for a small fire.

When the wood is gathered and her blood pumping again, she looks at Layrn's wounds. Already the bites and scratches have softened, gentled to a light red, a high contrast to their red, angry, bloody state just hours before.
Myra hugs Layrn tightly "Hang on my boy. You'll be alright."

Liana stands at the entrance to the castle, hugging her elbows. She can hear the thunder of hooves on cobblestones as the hunting party returns. She wipes away tears, knowing her sister will not be with them. Her heart imagines her laughing sister galloping around the corner on her elegant bay mare, Russet, grouse dangling from her saddle bags and her pup Layrn bounding clumsily before them, tongue lolling out behind him.
It is that last thought that breaks her reverie just as the hunting party returns, her father's grim face in the lead. The horses are panting and lathered in sweat. Just as they had planned. Just as they had cruelly thought out whilst her sister lived unawares of

her demise.

Gwen and Ariea burst from the castle, stopping short behind their eldest sister. Gwen cries out and Liana can hear Ariea sobbing. Frieda walks slowly up behind her sister and hugs her tightly. It is a burden they shall hold heavily in their hearts for the rest of their lives. Gwen and Ariea were spared the knowledge of when it would happen and how, but did it make their loss any less great?

When father had seen the powers that encompassed Myra, he had told them that the day would come that Myra would have to be sacrificed.

At least in the woods she might survive, safe from the Wulf hunters. If she stayed in the court, she would be sentenced to death and the kingdom brought to ruin. So, Belloc's daughters prepared her, knowing she might never make it out of those woods. Knowing they would never see their beloved sister again. From the age of five she had quietly been groomed for the day she would be sacrificed. It was dangerous. If Myra did survive then she could completely overturn the kingdom and undermine the king's authority. But father could not bring himself to let her powers be known, he couldn't lose her too, not after their mother had been killed. He hoped that if Myra never knew her powers then she would never have to be sacrificed. But as she grew so had the appearance of her powers. Liana had made it her mission to show her sister all the love and kindness she could spare so then Myra might hold onto it in the time ahead when she would have to survive alone. She only wished she'd had more time.

Their father hands his horse to a stable hand, his bow clutched in one hand and his helm resting under his arm. As he walks closer Liana can see the tracks of tears down his cheeks. "I'm sorry" he croaks, choking on a sob. Frieda runs to hug their father, both crying soundly in each other's arms. Liana cannot find comfort in him though, not after this. She cannot bare to hug her sister's killer. Even if he is her father. Her other sisters rush to their father. Clutching his wolf skin cloak as if drowning in sorrow so deep that they must find salvation.

Liana clutches her elbows so tight it makes her fingers white. Her father looks up at her, his blue eyes blurry, but hers are clear now. Clear and feral like a predator. She holds his gaze until he breaks it, then she turns and storms away into the castle. Hearing her children wailing for their mother down the hall. "Rest in peace dear sister, hold Layrn close in death. He will protect you."
She breathes, pushing down the anger and grief.

Her children, Susanna and Tico push against their nursemaids' strong arms, screaming for their mother. As Liana approaches her blond-haired children, she hears Susanna the eldest say, "If I can't have my mom then I want Myra! Myra takes care of us better than you!". She spits the words in the maids face. Liana swallows a lump in her throat, feeling suffocated by her grief.
When the nursemaid sees her, she apologizes profusely releasing the children as if scalded.

Susanna grabs her mother's skirts hugging the linen close to her chest as she looks up with her big blue eyes, "Where's Myra mommy? I want to show her my new dress!" Liana wipes at her eyes, holding her breath lest she give away the sob building in her chest. Tico tugs on her skirt, "What's wrong mommy? Why are you crying?" She hugs her children close.

"I'll be fine" Then she signals to the nursemaid and runs out of the room.

Frieda finds her in the kennels, sitting among the hounds, crying into the furs of the dogs surrounding her. The entire kennel is quiet, which is odd as the dogs are often heard howling even inside the castle's main dining room, situated in the middle of the palace.
Dogs sit quietly around Liana, leaving her space to pour out her

sorrow.

Although Myra and Liana had an age gap of seven years, they had been the closest to each other. Liana had spent the most time with Myra out of all the sisters. Liana and Myra had the kind of connection that none of the other sisters could ever hope to have with her. Frieda knew that when the time came for Myra to be sacrificed, it would be hardest for Liana to let her go.

Frieda steps gingerly into the kennels, dogs turn to her but are silent, their eyes filled with sorrow.

"Liana? Can I come in?"

Liana doesn't respond.

Mustering her courage, Frieda rushes to her, weaving through the hounds and wrapping her arms around her. Liana tries to push her off but as soon as Frieda backs away, she grabs her shoulders, pulling Frieda to her.

Her hold is tight, she pulls Frieda closer as if trying to tuck her away inside her heart.

"What have we done? WHAT HAVE WE DONE?!" She yells out into the sky. Her sobs make Frieda's heart break. But all she can do is hold her. Nothing they do now can bring Myra back. She's gone.

After a time, Liana's sobs grow quieter and the kennel master peaks his head in, Frieda looks him in the eyes and shakes her head. He slips out again.

"My Myra... my poor Myra... She'll never forgive us. I'll never forgive us." Liana gulps.

Frieda pulls away, pushing Liana up so I can look her in the eye. "Come now... Father wouldn't let her suffer. We did what we had to do and now it's done. Your husband will be worried, let's go inside and get you cleaned up."

She nods, wiping fiercely at her tears, her eyes red and puffy.

She stands with her back to Frieda. Liana heaves a great sigh and straightens her posture to that of the soon-to-be Queen that she is. When she turns her eyes are clear and harsh with anger.

"Come, let us get out of this place and leave the dogs in peace with their supper."

They leave and if anyone had seen her, they would have no idea the kind of pain she had inside. Only, a shiver might slip down their spine when they looked into Liana's cold, unwavering eyes.

Frieda and Liana had little troubles taking the direct route to Liana's chambers. Those that they passed moved like water in their wake. When they reached the door to Liana's chambers, Frieda gave her hand a gentle squeeze and walked on to her own chambers. Frieda could hear Liana's husband's deep gentle voice as he asked, "is there anything I can do?" Her murmured response was lost in the distance between them. *What was there he could do? What was there that anyone could do?* Myra was gone.

A few days have passed since the white wolf licked Layrn's wounds. Myra is on edge. For, every day since their arrival the wolves have surrounded them. Myra even saw a litter of pups playing on the outskirts of the group, yipping and playing. Layrn's strength has grown. His wounds have begun to disappear slowly. He still can't walk but he lifts his head and whacks his tail on the ground when he sees her. She can leave the circle of wolves to hunt or gather wood but is watched carefully by the pack. She always makes sure to leave an offering with the wolves, praying each time that her growing familiarity with them won't be her downfall.

To her surprise, trust seems to grow between them. When she settles down next to her fire, snuggled tightly beside Layrn she can hear the sighs of the wolves around her and her fear starts to subside.

Her mind whispers at night of danger in this trust. Wolves will forever be wild and unpredictable. They are not the hounds of her sister's kennels.

She awakes early this morning to the haunting howls of wolves. The wolves look restless, circling and whining, two wolves break the tension with a scrap, growling and snarling as they tumble about. The lead wolf breaks it up with a low snort. Then the pack sifts away into the forest. Myra leaps from her bed, trying to watch their departure, feeling suddenly very alone and vulnerable.

The wolves are gone. She can hear faint howls of excitement in the distance. "Probably just going off to hunt." She mumbles to herself, but her voice wobbles.

Layrn pants and gives her a big doggy grin. Myra crouches rubbing her fingers together, trying to ask him to come to her. He wags his tail fiercely, and brings his front paws up struggling to lift his bulk with his weak legs. He gets briefly into a half crouch and then collapses back onto his stomach. His eyes are big, and he scrabbles trying to lift himself up again, but Myra rushes to him. She strokes his soft fur, bringing her head close to his and whispering "Shh it's alright, just sit still Layrn". Tears begin to well in her eyes and she forces them back. This is not the time for tears. Once Layrn has settled she goes out into the forest and gathers more wood.

Days pass quickly. The snow begins to melt, making a fire even more necessary when the dampness seeps into the bones. The wood gets wetter, soggy from the melting snow and Myra fears for Layrn.

Layrn can move in small bursts, only walking around for a little while. His once thick, gleaming fur is now dull and hangs on him like a coat much too big. His muscles have wasted away from lack of use. His coat starts to shed as the days get longer and Myra saves as much fur as she can.

Myra's days are filled with the construction of a lean to. A warmer, drier shelter then the one she had. Layrn's fur becomes the insulation, along with leaves and twigs woven tightly together to keep the rain out.
The wolves return as Myra finishes the construction of her lean to.
The wolves begin to try and play with Layrn as his strength grows. But Myra runs them off, yelling at them.
Soon Layrn accompanies her on her treks. His muscles begin to fill out and his strength and hunger returns.

The wolves keep watch, but, grow more restless each day. Until one day the white wolf stands in front of Myra. The wolf's green-golden eyes bore into hers. Then, the wolf turns with a pointed glance back at Myra before trotting off to the pack.

The afternoon wears down with no sign of the wolves returning. Fear tightens in Myra's stomach. "The wolves are gone", The words slip from her tongue before her mind has registered them. Layrn looks up at her and whines.

The sun bids the land farewell, leaving the last brilliant rays shimmering on damp leaves and blinking through branches. Myra, with all her belongings upon her back, walks away from her newly built shelter. Layrn bounds ahead of her, oblivious to what she has done.

Estranged

"Your majesty, a certain Myra Wolfbern wishes an audience with you. I believe she may be coming for work in the kennels… As she has many dogs with her." The Queen nods her head in approval "Bring her in". The Queen's posture hides the weariness in her eyes.
Her hair is almost white with age, crow's feet nest in the corners of her eyes.
Prince Tico sits beside her, his golden mane of hair dazzling in his youth but, underneath the charm hides a quiet malice. Therefore, the old Queen will not give up her throne. Tico would be drunk on power and would bring ruin to the kingdom. Suzanna is already married to a powerful ally, safe… For now.
She motions and a servant brings her wine and cheese. The throne room doors clang open and the banter of many dogs accompanies it.
An old woman walks in, her skin darkened and dry from many years in the weather. With a flick of the wrist the old woman makes the room go quiet.
The dogs gather around her, silently watching the Queen's subjects standing on the outskirts. The dogs' eyes are feral, their gazes sending more than one shiver crawling down a spine in the great hall. They look like wolves, but, surely none would tame such foul creatures… Or would they?

A guard steps towards the old woman, scolding her for not bowing to the Queen. The woman doesn't look at him, instead, her gaze settles on the Queen's eyes. There's something hauntingly familiar about them. The woman before Liana, has dark, brown hair down to her knees. It is gathered into even dreadlocks like the medicine women of the south. Her skin is wrinkled and leathery, her hands are tattooed with symbols that are indecipherable in the folds of skin on her bony hands. When the woman speaks it sends a jolt through Liana. "I will not bow to my sister. We are equal and should greet each other as such." The guard looks towards the Queen searching for guidance. Liana flicks her hand and the guard steps away respectfully. She leans towards the old woman.

"And pray tell me, what sister would you be, when all lay dead beneath the ground?" Her voice constricts at the end. The pain of their loss will never be spoken of lightly.
The old woman looks as though struck through the heart. She bends her head, seeming to gather her wits about her. When she looks up into the Queen's eyes, it is not the feral, guarded look of before, but one of love and pain. Again, the Queen's mind scratches at a long-forgotten memory.
"Myrianna Martenlander...", The woman's breath wobbles, and she takes a gulp of air. "Fifth daughter of King Belloc of the Kingdom of Gandalon."
The Queen chokes, her gut wrenched by memory. "Myra?!" she croaks, then faints.

The palace is in an uproar when the Queen awakens in her bed. Her bones creak and she can feel the start of a back cramp that will probably paralyze her for a few hours if she doesn't have her tincture.
Beside her sits Tico, watching her intently as he fiddles with a dagger in his hands.
His eyes have taken on the dark, almost pupil-less look, they sometimes get when his mind has gotten away on him.
Liana lurches upright, yelling "Guards! Guards!" her mind is too foggy to think of anything else to warn them of a possible assassin.

A guard stumbles in, sword half unsheathed, looking startled from a pleasant nap.

Tico rises sheathing the dagger and smiles at the guard. "Nothing to worry about George, my mother was simply having a bad dream. I will leave you now. Good day, Mother." Tico sweeps from the room before the Queen can explain herself. The guard slumps against the door jamb breathing hard, as if recovering from a strong whack of adrenalin.

"Are you quite alright George?", the Queen asks quietly. The guard straightens.

"Perfectly, your majesty. Just gave me quite a fright there." He clears his throat remembering himself,

"Is there anything your majesty wishes of me, or should I return to my post?" The Queen shivers, looking frail among the large bedsheets. She suddenly looks very old and uncertain. A pang strikes the Guard's heart as he watches her gather herself. *Poor woman. She has lived through so much.* he thinks, before scolding himself for such thoughts. As if the Queen were able to read minds too.

"George... I need a private audience with you. Make sure the servants are out of this room and shut the door." He bows his head and ushers the servants out.

Standing uncertainly by the door he asks, "your majesty?".

She takes a deep breath.

"I... You have sworn an oath to protect me against all costs." He nods, not seeing where the conversation is going.

She bites her lip, "well... I do not... ugh. The prince... Prince Tico just... He is not to be trusted. Not in my chambers or in the kingdom. I want a guard placed on him and I want to be updated on his whereabouts and activities. I have reason to believe that if I hadn't woken when I did, that... That my son would have murdered me whilst I slept."

She began to shiver, her breath coming in hitches as she looked up at her guard. She looked so helpless. Her bony frame was obvious beneath her gown and the guard averted his gaze.

"Your majesty, I should be hung for allowing anyone with a

weapon into your chambers. I will place a double guard on you and Prince Tico, and I will not let anyone come in to see you without your expressed permission. I will do double shifts if it means that your majesty is safe and protected." Tears began to well in his eyes and he blinked them away. After composing himself, he met the Queen's eyes and saw tears there as well.
"Thank you, George. I will not be hanging you, for I'll need your loyalty if we are to keep Prince Tico from getting the throne." A ghost of a smile appeared on her lips before she became the strong, unyielding Queen that George was used to seeing.
"Now bring my servants in, I need to see if this woman is truly my sister. We may have a chance at conquering this throne once and for all, if none of us get assassinated beforehand." Then she nodded to the door and George left, servants replacing him almost immediately.

The Queen is swept into the throne room with ten guards about her. George among them, looking stern and worried at the same time. One day she will have to tell her captain of the guards to teach his men how to hide their emotions from their faces.
When she enters, the room goes quiet. Her subjects unlace themselves from their conversations and bow respectfully to her. Asking of her wellbeing. She replies with an "I'm fine, thank you for your concern", before sitting upon the ancient throne.
"Bring her in", she commands from the dais. The old woman enters again. Her dogs are silent behind her. This time she bows.
"I beg your pardon for creating such upset in your house. It was not my intention." She straightens and her eyes tell more than her words. The Queen dismisses her subjects, leaving only her sworn guards among her. "Tell me, what proof do you have that you are truly my sister, in blood, as well as name?" Myra stares into the Queen's eyes.
"Liana, do you remember the dog you gave me on my fifteenth birthday? Do you remember sharing your dreams of the future and laughing at my stupid jokes as you abandoned your duties for a few hours to sit with me among the hunting dogs? Do you

remember the way Layrn used to bound after the grouse when we went hunting with father?

Or, do you only remember my name, spoken of in secret after my exile. No one ever came looking for me; not you, not father, not even a single servant, in the hopes of catching a glimpse of my ghost among the trees.

What I can't believe, is that, after you took the throne, you let it continue. You told the village folk that they must sacrifice their fifth daughter to the Gods, so they might be graced with a son. Did you know that some had to sacrifice more than one child? Did you know that those children were left to die of exposure rather than be killed?! What proof do I have that I am your sister? I saved every child I could find for the last thirty years! I could have created an army to go against you, to take down the kingdom brick by brick.

Instead, I came alone. I came to tell you that you must stop this." The Queen bit her lip, keeping her face a mask of obscurity.

"Why did you wait so long?", she whispered. Her voice carried easily through the hall and among the silent guards. They held their breaths, listening for the answer.

Myra crumpled to her knees, the wolves surrounded her, licking at her face and whining quietly. She did not raise her head, when she whispered,

"I couldn't. I have asked myself, time and again, why didn't you go right away? Why didn't you stop this a long time ago? I have no answer. I was abandoned. I wasn't brave enough to confront father, or you, knowing I would probably be executed on the spot. But, I have nothing to lose now. I am an old woman, as are you. What difference does it make if I die now?" The Queen swiped tears from her eyes.

She croaked "Where did those you saved go?" Myra's head jerked up and her eyes seemed to burn with anger. "I gave them skills to survive in the wilderness and told them they could never go back to their homelands. They had to change their names and bury the lives that they had before. Some went to the south-

ern lands; others went east to the countries there. They would take off into the forest and I would never see them again. I do not know how many survived. But none came back and none stayed"
Her gaze burned into Liana's soul.

Liana stands and steps towards the old woman. Her guards rush to push them apart, but, the Queen motions them back.

"It's ok. I know her to be my sister. I will not leave her kneeling below my feet; I will not let her suffer again." The wolves, much like the guards raise their hackles and growl at the Queen. Myra shushes them and stands, waiting for her sister to step before her.

Both women stand rooted before each other. One pale with a golden crown upon wispy, white hair. Her body is frail and slim beneath her royal gown. The other, with dark brown hair in dreadlocks down her back, her skin leathery and tanned by years in the weather, cloaked in leathers and covered in an animal skin. They looked utterly different and yet, there was a spark of familiarity between them that only sisters could have.

"I thought you were lost to me forever", Liana's voice rasps out. Myra smiles, tears welling in her eyes,

"Did you really think I was that bad with a bow?" Liana laughs wetly, rubbing tears from her eyes and hugs her sister tightly.

Tico watches from the dais, his eyes are dark with anger. Anger that has boiled inside him since he was a little boy. A clingy jealousy, sneaks up his shoulders. His mother and Myra had always been close. Liana had never given him as kind words as she had with Myra. She had never given him the kind of attention he so desperately had sought for. Neither had his father ever given him any power or position with which to be proud of. Now, here was his long-lost aunt, that would swipe away all that he had worked for, with a smile and a sarcastic remark. He had to face the truth. Liana cared more about her sister than she did for him.

It wouldn't be all hugs and smiles for much longer. Not while he was still in court.

Clan of Wolves

It had taken Myra many days to find the wolves. Just as she had given up hope, she heard the lonely twin howls of the alphas. Their songs entwined together into the night. If her ears could prick forward like Layrn's, they would have.

She exchanged an excited glance with her dog. They ran towards the sound. Tripping in the deep snow as both paws and feet sunk in at unpredictable times. One step sinking low into the ground only to have the next, supported by the snow. They reached the top of a low hill within the forest. Before them was the pack, five adults and three pups. The alphas halted their howling duet to glare at them, suspiciously. Several of the other wolves encircled the pups. The white wolf stepped towards them, calculating their behavior.
Myra cursed herself, it was just as she had predicted. She had grown too familiar with the wolves, and now they were going to attack her.
But, they didn't.
Layrn gave a cheerful bark of greeting, and the wolves relaxed a hair. Myra took that as her opportunity to get a little distance between herself and the wolves.
She called Layrn, and they cautiously walked down the hill again. Retracing their steps to the bottom of the hill. She heard Layrn's paws crunching and punching through the snow. They wouldn't be able to go far in these conditions. They were in danger of cutting a leg on the crusty edges of the snow, not to mention the amount of energy it took to climb through the unpredictable snow.
Myra heard a second scrabbling of feet behind her, and she

whirled. There was the white wolf, again, struggling along behind her and Layrn.

The wolf seemed more curious than aggressive, as if she wondered where they were going to.

Myra had no clue where she was headed. She just needed some space between the wolves. She wanted a nice fire to dry her clothes against the wet and cold that had packed itself into the gaps in her boots. Her fur coat was close to useless now. She had attempted to make the skirt of her dress into pants, but it was now a tattered mess. She could feel a great hopelessness wash over her. There was no home with her among the wolves. She had left her own shelter far behind. Her only friend that remained was Layrn. The white wolf was still following them. Frustrated, tired, and defeated, Myra whipped around, startling the wolf back a couple steps. "WHAT DO YOU WANT!?" Myra yells at the wolf. The wolf blinks up at her, confused.

"Why are you following us?" The words fall out quietly, settling on the snow between them. The wolf looks into her eyes and wags her tail uncertainly. Her look is much like Layrn, when he doesn't understand why she is angry. The emotions raging in her stomach come to a boil. "I've been thrown out by your pack. I've been thrown out by mine. I left everything I've built far behind, to follow you. What do you want from me?" Tears blur her vision. "I can't offer any food or shelter or... or anything. I have nothing to give."

The wolf pants happily and struggles up to her. It sits in front of her making Layrn's hackles raise. He lets out a low grumble. The wolf batts it's nose on Myra's hand. Slowly, carefully, Myra puts out her hand to pet it. The wolf pushes its head against her hand. Stunned, she gently strokes it's head. The wolf's piercing eyes close in contentment, and it rubs against her. Myra laughs uncertainly. Then, as quickly as it came, it trots back to the pack. It wags its happily. Layrn relaxes slightly, and goes over to Myra. He leans against her, his favorite way of reassuring himself that she's still there.

They make camp a little way from the ridge where the wolves are. Myra settles in front of a tiny, sputtering fire, and waits. A thin shelter lays behind her. A combination of branches and fallen logs hastily slapped together.

She stays there for days. Each day she heads into the forest to hunt. Each day she returns with fewer arrows. Eventually, she returns with only the bow, barely strong enough to hold herself up.

Myra has no food, but the hunger has subsided by now. Her thin frame is obvious below the fur coat. Her stomach is swollen with the beginnings of starvation. *What was the point of going on? Layrn could find a place among the pack. She could die in peace, knowing that no one would be saddened by her death... But, what about the other children? The others abandoned to the Gods. How could she stop them from perishing too?* Myra is startled from her reverie by the sound of paws struggling through snow. She lifts her head, staring blindly into the darkness. Her tired eyes try to focus on the creature before them. Layrn's vision is much stronger than hers and he growls menacingly. The 'yip yip' of a wolf follows the sound. Layrn backs up slightly. Then, Myra's eyes focus on the wolf before them. It drags what looks like a half-eaten deer haunch towards them. This wolf is not the white one that healed Layrn, but instead the Alpha male. His coat is charcoal black with white tips on the end of his fur, creating a fascinating variance to his coat. His muzzle holds grey amidst the black and reveals scars from old fights. Yet, he does not look old as he stands before them. He grumbles, looking first at Layrn, then Myra. Unlike the white wolf he does not stare into their eyes. His size is impressive. He is larger than Layrn, standing as high as Myra's waist. The alpha blinks at them for a moment, bumps the haunch, and struggles back up to the ridge again. Myra stares after him. She tries to imagine the wolf's plan, to bring the haunch down to them.

Layrn bounds over to the haunch, and tears into it. Myra yells

at him to leave it alone. She pulls him off it. Bringing out her bone knife, she cuts jagged pieces from the haunch. If they could smoke it, it could last them a while. Especially since the cold was starting to seep away, with the longer days.
Myra attempts to build up the fire. She jigs up a spit to cook on. She could cook enough for her and Layrn tonight then bank the fire until it's mostly smoke, then put the rest of the meat on that. She looks at the haunch. Thankfully, with the cold, no bugs crawl in it. Its already starting to look like it's reached its end. She must smoke it well, otherwise they will be sick from it. But, even as those plans roll through her head, her stomach speaks a different tune. Her shrunken belly growls angrily at her. Before she realizes it, she's ripped the meat off the fire, and she has it in her mouth. She freezes. She'd heard of those near-starving, killing themselves, by eating too much She rips the chunk in half. Returning the other half to the skewer again. She breathes deeply, trying to overcome her hunger. She will survive these woods. If she can make it past this hunger, she will survive.

Weeks pass, the wolves continue to bring her meat. Myra's stomach grows again, her legs and arms flesh out. Spring has come. Mud replaces snow and the sun begins to shine more strongly.
Myra's tattered coat gets left behind when the pack moves again. She will have to find a fur this spring, to keep her warm next winter. Each time the wolves stay put for more than a day, Myra cuts a notch in a tree. If the wolves continue to stay at the same few dens each time of the year, then she can build a more permanent shelter at each spot. Then, maybe, she can find her way out of these woods and back home.

The need for shelter grows less as the heat of spring blossoms.

The wolves keep watch on her, and begin to play with Layrn as one of their own. The white wolf often comes to Myra for attention. How strange that a wolf would enjoy these things.

It is a day such as this, Myra sits below a cedar tree, watching the wolves play. An unusual sound erupts from the forest. A kind of screech unlike any birds in the forest. The wolves hear it too, and stop. They listen again for the sound, but it has changed now. The call sounds angrier. Almost like a human cursing. Myra has thought many times, that bird calls were people. The crows and magpies were the worst for those things. They had such bizarre calls that seemed to continuously change. It was hard to identify their sounds as bird calls.
This was different though. Myra stands, Layrn sidling up beside her. They walk towards the noise.

As they grow nearer, the sounds become more distinct. Myra knows that its a human. Her legs begin to run of their own accord; she scrambles through brush and over logs, desperate to get to them. She can hear their wails loudly now, as she stumbles into a small clearing amidst the brush. The wails stop abruptly. Before her crouches a small girl maybe five or six years old. She has no clothes upon her body and her hair is a wild, tangled jungle upon her head. Her body is smeared with dirt and her feet are bleeding from walking on the hard ground. Myra crouches, trying to drag words, scraping up from her throat. It has been five months since she last saw another human being. Five months since she spoke to anyone but herself. "It's okay! I'm not going to hurt you." The girl hides her face, sobbing into her arms. Myra can only imagine how terrifying she must look, having been in these woods so long. "Hey, it's okay! I'm here to help you... What's your name?" Myra inches closer, careful to keep Layrn's large, boisterous self away from the girl, so as not to frighten her.
The girl snuffles, "I'm Julia... Who're you?", she glares at Myra fiercely.
"I'm Myra. Come, let me look at your feet. Are you hurt anywhere else?", Julia unfurls herself plopping down on her butt with her feet pointed towards Myra.

"I'm hungry", the girl whines quietly.

Myra smiles "Well, that's something I can fix easily enough!". The girl's soles are scraped. It's hard for Myra to tell how deep some of the cuts are, without cleaning them off.

"I'm going to carry you over to the river. I need to get these clean, so I can see how best to heal your wounds." Myra says, reaching under the girl to pick her up. Julia wraps her legs around Myra's middle as easily as if they were sisters. Myra carries the girl, feeling self-conscious and awkward carrying a naked girl. Being the younger sister, she had little experience with kids. The occasional time that she cared for Liana's children, they had always been withdrawn with her. They didn't trust as easily as this girl.

The river was icy cold from the new tendrils of spring. Its banks were steep and washing away from the high river. Large stones kept parts of the bank intact.

The rocks were covered in slippery moss and algae. It let out a calming ssshhhh and woosh as the water flowed down the river. Myra propped the little girl on a rock, clambering closer to the fast-flowing water. The river wasn't very wide, but, it moved like it was escaping a banshee.

Cupping water in her hands, Myra scrambles back to the girl. Her fingers already feel numb. How irritating it was that no matter how tightly you squished your fingers, or how much your hands overlapped, the water always found a way to dribble out so quickly. Myra dropped her hands over the girl's feet. Creating a gasp of shock, and a little wail from Julia.

"I'm sorry. I know the water's cold. But this will help." Julia nodded, her eyes brimming with tears. Myra did this twice more. Then she gently wiped the cuts as best she could with her fingertips. The cuts weren't severe but would sting awfully for a few days. Gathering moss and some paper birch, they took off back to the wolf pack.

Myra explained to Julia her connection with the wolves as they went. She didn't want the girl to be scared when they came upon the pack. Myra just hoped that the wolves would allow her to bring Julia in.

Myra strode next to Liana as they entered the ban
quet hall. The Queen's subjects scrambled to their feet. Liana hadn't had her presence announced beforehand. She preferred to catch her subjects in the act of being themselves. She didn't do it all the time, so as not to arouse suspicion, that she did this on purpose. A group of knights continued to laugh and joke with each other, oblivious to the Queen's presence. They conversed most-casually, sitting in a man spread with their arms about each other, jostling each other and making their drinks spill upon the table. Tico stood behind the Queen, staring daggers into her back. Liana's face registered the briefest of smiles, before her page boomed out in his deep voice,
"I announce Queen Liana of Gandalon, Prince Tico, and Lady Myra of the-". Here the page faltered, glancing worriedly at Myra. She grinned and whispered,
"Of the wolf clan." The page quickly turned back
"Ehm. Lady Myra of the wolf clan", He bowed hurriedly to the Queen and swept out of the room, having to hold his hat to keep it from falling off in his swiftness. The knights turned, eyes wide, and quickly rushed to their feet, some knocking over their stools in the process. They bowed deeply; their faces flushed with embarrassment.

Liana swept through the room, appearing to float over the floor. Myra was none so graceful. Too many years spent surviving in the forest had erased her lessons of sweeping through a room. She walked with long strides, her arms swinging. It was obvious to the subjects that she was unused to court life and the affects her long strides had on the beauty of a dress. No one would have mocked her for it. It was immediately apparent in her mannerism that she had just as much power as the Queen. Tico huffed in annoyance and strolled languidly behind them.

Whispers flew up like leaves on a breeze as they took in Myra.

"How did a medicine woman of the southlands manage to get a place among the Queen's table?",

"I've never heard of any wolf clans in the south",

"But, she definitely has the ceremonial hair from the southlands.",

"Maybe she's one of the elders that doesn't come to court much?",

"Who knows!"

Myra smiled; amused. The court was much the same as it had been when she was a girl. Gossip formed and flew about like the murmurations of starlings in the sky.

Broken

Myra carried Julia in her arms as she took long, lumbering steps up the ridge to the wolves. Layrn yipped excitedly and bounded before her, chasing a young wolf in a game of tag. When Myra reached the top, the wolves yipped and barked, surrounding her in joyous greeting. They stopped short as they smelled the Julia, then they backed away grumbling. The Alpha male, whom Myra had begun to call Traveler because of his nature of constantly forcing the pack to move, stepped forward; his posture aggressive, ears forward and tail erect. He bared his teeth, his eyes and nose moved, about trying to understand the scent of the other human. Then, he barked and leaped up, slamming all four feet onto the ground with tremendous force. Myra was so startled she fell over, Julia collapsing with her. They both scrambled to their feet, watching the other wolves. The wolves watched them; their glares apparent beneath their thick brows.
Myra crouched, holding Julia tightly to her chest. The girl was quietly sobbing, Myra could smell her fear.
Myra's eyes filled as she blurted, "I'm sorry! I didn't mean to upset you. I just - She…. She needed help. You would help your own kind if they were in need… Wouldn't you?" But she knew that wolves did not do things like humans. If a wolf wasn't part of the pack they would very rarely be invited in, especially if they were injured. Myra swept her tears away.
"Come on Julia, we need to give them some space." Hurt, Myra turned away crying. There was Layrn, standing perplexed among the young pups. One still lay on its back playfully. It wagged its tail when it spotted her. The Alpha female cuffed it with her nose.
"Layrn, come on", Myra's voice cracked. This was the one family

she had felt she could trust. The only ones who hadn't abandoned her. Now they had thrown her out, like some mangy dog bringing disease. Layrn followed her, sobering at her expression.

Myra spent the afternoon hunting. The little girl clung to her back. She was oddly silent for a young child. Layrn sniffed the deer-trail ahead. He'd learned it was his job to flush out the prey. He would lead Myra to the kill, then watch proudly as she would take it down. Today he ran ahead of them, excitedly searching the trails. Myra continued to wipe away tears, trying to focus on the task ahead of them. Eventually Julia whispered in Myra's ear,

"Was that your family? What happened? Why won't they let you join them?", Myra stifled a sob. Rubbing her fingers along the soft wood of her bow, she whispered back,

"The wolves are all I have left." Suddenly, Layrn leaped from the bushes, wagging his tail excitedly, doing his best not to bark. Myra hiked Julia up further on her back, and they trotted into the bush. When they grew close, Layrn began to slink across the ground, gathering himself for the pounce. Myra quietly dropped Julia off her back and knocked an arrow to her bow. Tip toeing closer, Myra saw a group of grouse kicking away in the underbrush, completely oblivious to Myra and Layrn. Drawing back her bow, Myra aimed. The grouse looked up, staring into the distance. Fump! The arrow hit its mark. An explosion of feathers followed the impact and the other grouse took to the skies, flying blindly into the tree canopy. Layrn leaped and caught the leg of one. It squawked, flapping madly, before Layrn killed it. When the commotion died down. Myra retrieved her grouse. she could hear Julia crying quietly behind her. She turned to Julia, who crouched in the underbrush, her head resting in her knees. Myra bent down and touched Julia's arm. The girl flinched glancing up at her wide eyed. "You killed it! You're a murderer!", she spat.

Myra blinked. "I'm hunting. We need food to survive. I didn't kill it without reason."

Julia stopped crying and seemed to think about this for a moment. Then she looked up at Myra, her bright blue eyes searching her face.

"Are you going to hunt me?", she asked seriously.

Myra laughed,

"No! of course not! Don't be silly". She holds out her hand and Julia takes it. Bending down so that Julia can get on her back, Myra says,

"Come on, let's go roast this grouse and get some food in our tummies. I'm starving!" Julia leaps on her back, mimicking a growling stomach.

Flames licked at the spitted grouse, as if trying to taste it. The orange glow of the fire played with the shadows that lay upon Myra's face. The moon was rising, a full orb in the dark sky.

Myra's heart was heavy despite the final company of another human. After close to a half year on her own, it was strange for Myra to suddenly have this company. She struggled with the warring emotions inside her.

Then, a lonely wolf howl drifted up to the sky. It was followed by another, then another, until the whole pack could be heard in the song. The wolves' sorrow radiated through the forest that night. To Myra it felt as though they sang straight from her heart. She wished for nothing more than to have the pack surround her and keep her protected.

In Myra's dreams that night, she saw the white wolf. It was standing over her, and in the dream, the wolf's golden eyes were close, searching her own. She heard it's voice in her mind.

"Where are you Wolfborn? We need you."

Myra woke with a start. Layrn lifted his head from his paws, watching her. She scrambled to him, hugging him tightly. Feeling an itchy tingling at the base of her skull that made her want to crawl out of her skin.

Julia awoke soon after, complaining of hunger. Myra cleaned up their camp, then checked and cleaned Julia's feet. The scrapes and blisters had healed over, but the skin was still tender. Myra used the remaining cloth from her bedroll to make the little one some shoes.

By mid-morning they had set out, the words of the white wolf echoing in Myra's mind. Julia was quiet as they maneuvered through the forest. Layrn bounded before them, excited for the day's journey ahead.

They were navigating a steep hill when the wind carried a distant howl.

"Yiojn?" Myra whispered, then blinked. Where had *that* name come from? Layrn answered with his usual loud bark. The howl grew excited and Layrn barked again.

They heard the quiet thud of paws galloping across the ground, then from the underbrush came the white wolf. When she caught sight of them, she yipped and barked happily, dancing in the way that only dogs can.

Julia hid behind Myra, clutching to her leg as Myra watched wolf and dog playfully tackle each other in greeting. Myra could feel the joy emanating from the wolf, but something troubled her. *Where was the rest of the pack? Why had they not rushed through the underbrush behind the white wolf?*

The wolf then greeted her, leaning against her legs like Layrn. She panted happily while Myra scratched her back. The wolf's fur was thick and lustrous. Strong wiry guard hairs rasped Myra's fingertips as she dug her fingers through the thick, soft undercoat that insulated the wolves so well.

After a while Julia unclutched herself from Myra's leg and peered around her wanting to reach for the wolf but afraid of what it might do. The wolf looked deeply into Julia's eyes and something connected between them. When Julia raised her hand toward the wolf, it bumped its nose against her. They both seemed to enjoy the magnificence of the connection. Julia laughed and the wolf bent into a playful crouch. Then they were off, bounding through the forest, Julia's sore feet and hunger forgotten in the moment.

Myra watched, bewildered as wolf and child played. Layrn soon joined them and got Myra going too. Myra was finally able to relax. After so long she could finally find space to play, without a care in the world.

They played like that for some time. The sun had reached its zenith when she heard the howls of the pack. She heard the thump of horse hooves and the howling of hunting dogs. They all stopped, their hearts in their throats.

Men shouted and she could hear the vicious snarling of a fight. They all began to run towards the commotion. When Myra finally made it through the underbrush, she saw the men galloping after a black wolf. Traveler was keeping the men off the rest of the pack by leading them away. Yiojn the white wolf hunched in the underbrush below Myra. She was whimpering. The rest of the pack could not be seen but Myra guessed they were hiding. Then she heard a sound that made her heart want to stop. It was the yelp of the injured. She peered out of the brush to try to see Traveler, but, between hunting dogs and the men on horseback, she couldn't see him.

Julia clung to her, one hand tightly in Layrn's fur and the other clutching to Myra's hand.

Myra tried to see the men on horseback. They looked familiar, but she couldn't see their insignias. Then one turned. On his shoulders draped the skin of a grey wolf, its thick fur soft and shimmering in the sunlight. His face was covered in a neat brown beard and upon his head lay a crown. Myra felt the breath leave her in a great gulp. There was her father, only a yard away, oblivious to her existence.

"Did you kill it Baird?", he shouted over the noise of the hounds.

Baird was her cousin, soon to reach his 18th birthday. This was not a hunt for food but a rite of passage into manhood. All men of the royal family had to pass this rite in order to be considered a man. Baird was late in this passage. He had never been very good with a bow and had taken this hunt several times before, when Myra had still been in the kingdom.

"Yes, my lord. Shot it right through the heart. The pages are just getting the hounds off it." Myra heard Julia gasp. She quickly covered the girl's mouth and they slunk off a little way. Myra pulled Yiojn away with all her strength.

"It's too late Yiojn, he's dead. There's nothing we can do for him." she whispered. Myra took them to a large thicket of blackberry bushes.

"Stay here. I'm going to see where they're taking him. Keep Yiojn with you, Julia. I'll be right back" Myra ran quickly back to the men. Her bow still rested comfortably in her hands. It would be an easy feat to kill the king in these woods. She knew them much better than he. But, she discards the thought. It would not solve anyone's problems if she did that. Climbing a tree, she looks out to the horsemen below. They had taken the hounds off Traveler. He lay there, an arrow embedded deep in his chest. His black coat smeared darker with blood.

"Now this one is a wolf to be proud of killing. He looks like a fine specimen. And there aren't many black wolves in these parts. It's a great honor to kill such a beast as this"

Myra heard her father say as Baird dismounted his horse and inspected the wolf.

"It's a shame the hounds got to him first. His coat has some punctures in it. But the pelt is salvageable." Baird motions for one of his guards to take the wolf. The guard lifts Traveler, removing the arrow. The wolf is larger than the guard, and he seems to struggle for a moment to lift the wolf. Myra's throat clutches

"This can't be real!" she breathes. Traveler's head lolls as he is thrown onto a pack horse. The animal's eyes roll as it catches wind of the wolf. It stands as they strap the carcass on. Traveler's golden eyes stare; growing glassy with death. His tongue hangs loosely out of his mouth, his teeth bloody.

Then, the troop of men head out again, Myra's father yelling out orders.

Just like that. Traveler is gone. Her father took yet another life away from her.

Myra's eyes blur again and she knuckles the tears away, but the sobs she can't control. She knows that she won't be able to climb down the tree in the state she's in. A chipmunk sits close to her, a pinecone in its jaws. Its innocent curiosity of her, ultimately breaks Myra down. "I'm so sorry Traveler! I'm so sorry." Myra sits in the tree for a long time, staring absently at the roughened earth where Traveller had laid. Scratch marks and paw prints of the hunting dogs disturbing the forest floor.

After a while Julia calls out,

"Myra! Myra, where are you?!"

Myra tries to compose herself, yelling shakily,

"I'm over here, in a tree. I'm coming down."

Julia rushes through the bush towards her

"Yiojn disappeared! I can't find her and I... I didn't know when you were coming back." Julia starts to cry. Myra clambers down the tree. Enfolding Julia in her arms.

"It's alright. I'm here now. I'm not going to leave you again. I'm sorry I left" Myra's eyes wander over Julia's head to see Layrn sitting behind the girl, his liquid brown eyes looking at hers. His tail wags lightly at her gaze.

Myra lifts Julia, propping her on her hip. She wipes the tears from the girl's face.

"Come on, let's go look for the pack. I want to know they're ok." Julia nods and wraps her legs tightly around Myra. Myra realizes distantly that they both are clothed in ripped up shreds of clothes. It was past time for Myra to begin replacing and making clothes for winter.

Myra cups a hand to her mouth imitating a wolf howl, Julia laughs despite herself.
"What are you doing?!" Myra closes her eyes, listening. "I'm trying to find the pack. I figure if I can get them to howl back, we'll be able to locate them. Come on let's hear your best wolf howl"
Julia tries to mimic Myra's howl but begins laughing halfway through. Layrn takes up the call, his howl eerie and very real.
Soon they hear the quiet sorrowful reply of the alpha female. After this long, Myra could pick out each individual from their barks and howls.
Julia squirms out of Myra's arms and they both make their way towards the sound.

Layrn finds the pack first and yips excitedly, galloping off further into the woods. Myra and Julia finally catch up. Pushing through brambles, they come upon the pack.
The wolves sniff Layrn, stiffly watching for any changes in his behavior. When they see Myra and Julia, their hackles raise. The alpha female bares her teeth. She is a greyish brown wolf, smaller than Traveler had been but still dwarfing Layrn. Her pups, now almost a year-old stand behind her, varying colors of black and grey. Myra could never find a name appropriate for the female. She was charismatic in the most beguiling way. She wasn't easy to understand or trust. The brown wolf, Quiern, the omega of the group, circled behind them. Layrn could feel the tension, but knew it wasn't directed at him.
Myra lowers her head submissively, motioning for Julia to do the same.
"I don't think they will trust us for a while. I don't want them to go out of my sight. We'll have to measure our steps carefully; one wrong move could cause us real harm. I don't want to scare them, but I won't leave them alone and risk the hunters coming back." Julia nodded and they backed away a few steps. The pack seemed to control their anger for the moment, but Quiern watched them stolidly. The alpha female whined; her body close to the ground now. Her pups surrounded her and

licked her muzzle, seeming to comfort her. Iko, a lanky grey wolf, howls; his voice feels like it goes right to the soul. Myra listens for a reply in the woods. No answer. *Where did you go, Yiojn?* Layrn joins the pack, who accept him readily. He sits among the wolf pups, looking like a protective uncle as the pups bite at his ears and paw at him.

Julia and Myra sit under a tree a few yards away and watch the pack. "Do you think she'll come back?" Julia asks quietly, holding her breath as if to keep from crying.

"Yiojn can take care of herself. She's a strong girl" Myra's words sound fake to her ears. She hugs Julia, comforting the girl.

Wolfborn! Where are you?

Myra startles, looking around. She exchanges glances with Julia, "Did you say something?"

Julia's brow furrows "No."

Wolfborn! Do not leave the pack. The hunters will come back and you must keep the pack safe!

"Who are you?" Myra calls into the wood.

Julia looks at her strangely.

"No one's here Myra... I'm scared" She clutches tightly to Myra. Myra comes back to herself.

"Don't worry, Julia. I just thought I heard something"

Myra listens. No more words come. She thinks of Yiojn, alone and confused in the woods, mourning the loss of her leader. Myra imagines her heart opening and sending a tendril of love towards her, she whispers,

"Come home, Yiojn. We miss you."

Yiojn

Yiojn had heard the thump of the arrow hit flesh. She had heard the yip of his pain. But, she could not save him from the humans. The men rode upon the horse prey like coyotes escaping the kick of an elk. The horses were not afraid; not afraid of the arrows they threw about. The pack could have taken down a horse like the ones the men rode. But instead the men on horseback had killed her sire. Yiojn had only known life with him and Echo as the alphas.

When she saw them drape his body over the horse's back, she couldn't take it anymore. His eyes had lost the soul within them, and no breath escaped his mouth. Never again would she hear his howl. Never again could she feel his calming presence, or trust in his guidance to move them where the men would not hunt them.

He was gone and the pack was split open like a walnut smashed to the ground. Yiojn could feel his spirit, restlessly roaming, trying to find his body again. She could feel the fear, could sense the unease of his soul. "Rest, Traveler. Your body fails you now. Have no fear, for soon you will join the moon's spirit and can watch over us there." She spoke as the magic within her grew, sending calming energy to his spirit. His spirit touched down and became whole for a moment. She could see the black wolf before her. His head was low and his tail was held between his legs. His golden eyes stared into hers though and he let out a howl. The howl was silent, only the motion remained. Yiojn could see his breath in a cloud of grey steam. Then, he disappeared. The only thing left was the cloud of breath, which dissipated.

She ran towards it. It was too late. The air was just as clear here

as it had been moments before. "Goodbye, old one", she whimpered. Setting out on a journey to stop the killings. She could not let it happen again. She heard the distant howls of the pack. Echo's was muted in a way, dissolute of feeling. She could not go back now. Someone would have to keep the pack safe while she searched for answers. The Wolfborn. She would protect them. She had smelled of recognition and betrayal when the men had come. She would keep the pack safe. The distance would be too far, and the girl would never understand her howl. So drawing on the wisdom of nature she yelled out with her mind,
"Wolfborn! Where are you?" The response was one of confusion, however, she sensed that the Wolfborn was close to the pack. *"Wolfborn! Do not leave the pack. The hunters will come back and you must keep the pack safe!"*
With a sigh, Yiojn set out at a trot, following the scent of the horses. She tried to ignore the blood spots that wreaked of the recent dead.

Myra stalks through the woods, her last arrow trained on the neck of a buck. Layrn and the other wolves lie nearby in the scrub. Julia stands beside her watching Myra intently. This will be Julia's teaching. The next time they take a kill it will be Julia with the bow in her hand. The excitement grows within Myra. The buck is healthy and young, a perfect kill that will last them some time. "May my heart guide me straight" Myra breathes out as the arrow shoots towards the deer. It hits square in the throat and the wolves leap from the bushes, biting at it and trying to take it down. If they can fall it then the carcass will be theirs, if not the deer may still get away from them and die off where they cannot find it. The arrow had shot true but it wouldn't kill it instantly. That was where the wolves came in.

The deer gave a mighty fight, but the wolves' hunger won out. It went down with a loud crash and a grunt. Then the hunt was over. Myra sent love to it, thanking it for the food and life it would bring them. *I give my life for yours now, strong one. Bear it wisely.* Myra stopped, stunned. She looked at the deer and its eyes gave the briefest of acknowledgments before they glazed over in death. She had to push the wolves off to get to the meat before they demolished it.

Julia ran into the woods and she could hear her vomiting.

"Poor girl." she murmured, slicing into the deer. The antlers would make some fine knives for the winter. She tried to skin a section of the meat but, had no idea how to cure it.

"This is pointless." She growled, throwing the tattered section of hide to the ground. Stomping back into the woods, the words she had heard echoing inside her head. She found Julia nearby. She was shivering, her eyes dazed.

"Julia?" Myra scuffed her foot along the ground, trying to break her from her daze.

"It's ok now. The deer is gone. He didn't suffer... Julia it's alright."

Julia glared at her, her eyes red and puffy from tears.

"Go away you *monster*! I don't ever want to see you again. Leave me alone!" Then Julia pushed past her and ran into the forest.

"JULIA! Julia... I didn't mean to upset you. Come back." Julia continued into the woods, disappearing into the underbrush.

"JULIA!" no answer.

"Bloody bones!" Myra carried the meat back to the den, picking up twigs along the way. The wolves were still feasting, so the den was empty and silent. She began to build a fire

"I'll find her once I have this meat over the fire." she told herself, but her eyes kept darting to the forest and her heart seemed permanently lodged in her throat.

She tried to focus on the task at hand but could not get the fire to start. Cursing, she whistled to Layrn. Nothing. She gave a quick howl. The forest was eerily silent "LAYRN! COME HERE BOY!" The hair on the back of her neck rose. Her feet were already running before the thought had even entered her mind.

"LAYRN... IKO... QUIERN!" She screamed, already panting from the adrenalin rushing through her. She bounded through the forest, leaping over logs. Her hair caught on a wild rose bush and she screeched, yanked back by the thorns. Ripping the lock off the bush, she ran faster, screaming for the wolves. They came bounding from the kill, perplexed and startled. Layrn ran to her, whining at her unease. Everyone was there. No one was hurt.

"Oh, thank the Gods!" she breathed, her knees buckling and tears welling from her eyes.

"Thank the Gods you're alright!" She dug her fingers into Layrn's fur, her mind wanting to scoop him up into her heart so he would forever be safe there. Safe from the arrows of her father's bow.

The wolves barked and yipped, picking up on her anxiety then realizing there was nothing the matter they returned to their kill.

Yiojn followed the scent of the horses long into the night. Her stomach gnawed at her like a pup on a bone. "shush" she whispered to it.

"You grow soft with all this abundance of the summer. Soon it will be winter, and food will be scarce. Mind you don't forget it!"

Her footpads felt a strange numbness to them. She guessed it was from the hours of trotting along the trail. It was so easy to stalk this prey. They scarcely looked behind them and left their scent like a beacon to the nose. She could follow them far across the land and they would never be the wiser.

The moon blinked out from behind the clouds and she could see ahead that the forest trees dwindled, and some were cut by those fang tools that the men used to bring the trees down. She could feel her hackles raise. Never in her life had she been this close to man. She had seen but once, the fang tools and the ravaged land. Never to this extreme.

For miles, the only thing that covered the ground were the dead stumps. You could hop from one to the next easily, the trees had grown so close together.

She could hear the man hunters long before she saw their fires. They rested in a sheltered place between two hills, where father wind would not tear at their clothes and whistle through their ears like it did everywhere else that the trees were cut. Yiojn felt exposed, her white coat was never good for blending in, except during the winter. Iko's coat was much better in these parts but he would never have the guts to follow a pack of men like these. Wolf hunters. She had been warned of these men as a pup, that was why unlike other wolves they never went after livestock when the food was scarce.

Hiding in the remaining scrub brush she watched the men. Perhaps if she could listen to the emotions in their voices she might be able to understand why they hunted her kind. They never used her kin's meat. She had heard a tale from Echo of her last mate who had brutally fought the men, trying to scare them off from hunting their pack. He had been killed, his body skinned and the meat of his body, along with the bones were tied up in a tree as an example. Echo would never have let Yiojn go near these men if she knew. But like Echo's mate, Yiojn would not let it continue. She could see the men laughing and hitting each other playfully. They wreaked of the poison they called alcohol. She could see how it affected them. Their speech slurred and their movements were jerky and uncoordinated. Why would they enjoy getting drunk on such stuff? If it affected them so much weren't they worried that they would kill themselves?

Yiojn could smell a familiar scent among the men. It was similar to the Wolfborn but different. She could pinpoint it to a man who stood at the edge of the fire. Other men in similar coats sat or stood near him, seeming on alert. She could tell he was the alpha of the group. He held an air about him that said he was in charge. He was a large creature, robust in bone and muscle, if a little on the chubby side. "Summer's been good to him too." she mused. He had a lot of facial hair, which was something Yiojn had never seen before. But it looked as though he kept it well groomed. Other men around him had similar problems on their faces. *Perhaps its something to do with their gender, or they have a terrible disease... It could explain the reason for them poisoning themselves. If they were going to die anyway it might as well be doing something that made them joyful.* And joyful they were. Laughing and disturbing the night with their loud voices.

She could see the horses tied up on two of the few remaining trees in the area. They looked unsettled, they kept shifting about and occasionally bumping into each other. A horse on the end nickered into the night. Its voice ringing out over the expanse of the land. Its call told that it was worried about a storm that lay on the horizon. They were exposed to the elements and the predators. It was worried of what might happen. Another horse, a black stout one, nickered back that all would be fine. It had been out on this range before and the hills would protect them from the worst of it. It exuded an air of confidence that calmed the other horses.

Yiojn grew tired of watching the horses. She could see the men were growing weary and some had already dropped off into sleep.

She waited, bleary eyed with exhaustion, as the last one finally dropped.

She crept into a dreamless sleep like a pup would next to their dam's warm belly.

Morning fluttered with the final bats returning to their den. The sun had not yet risen and a faint glow permeated the land.
Yiojn could hear the men snoring loudly. She snorted quietly in amusement and went in search of field mice. It would be sometime before the men finally woke. Their horses were hungry when they did. They hobbled the horses and let them graze the rough brush that covered the desolated land. Yiojn had to hide. If she was caught, they might decide to kill her, too. She sneezed at the thought of her hide gracing the shoulders of one of these disgusting humans.
The sun had been up for some time, when the men rode out. They sang celebratory songs and patted Traveler's killer on the back. He was a younger man than the Alpha male, yet not as young as some of their guards.
He sat proud in his saddle but had no concept of empathy for the animal underneath him. He wrenched the reins several times, while the horse, excited by the coolness of the morning pranced under him. She could feel the frustration building in the horse. Yiojn panted happily. How satisfying it would be if that man were bucked off and taught some humility from the animal that was burdened by his weight. She trotted along behind them, careful to stay downwind of the horses so they wouldn't spook at her scent.
Far away she could hear the faintest howl of Echo. Echo's voice cracked in the cold air as she called for Yiojn. Yiojn's heart pulled her homeward and she could feel Echo's voice sinking into that place in her heart that longed so much for the way things used to be. She took a deep sigh.
I'm safe Shadow mother, I will come back to you. She sent the thought out, it felt as though it caught on the breeze and blew straight to Echo. Shadow mother was the name she and her littermates had called Echo. How long it had been since Yiojn had

called her that.
Then with her heart heavy, Yiojn took off loping behind the man hunters. Fear rising as she caught wind of the kingdom and the many people who lived there.

Myra

Yiojn did not return to the pack. Myra had searched for her; the pack had howled for her.

No response came.

The pack moved again; this time deeper into the woods. They risked not being able to find as many deer and elk but, if they stayed, they might be hunted again.

Myra wished with all her might that she could take down those men. They had killed her hope, had stolen her salvation, and had damaged her relationship to the only family she had left.

The wolves would not come near Myra. Despite their recent hunt together, they would snap and growl at her if she got too close. So, when the pack moved on, she stayed behind. She still had to find Julia. It had been more than a few days since the little girl had disappeared into the woods and Myra was afraid she could be injured. Layrn was reluctant to leave the pack again but, he stayed by her side. He was the only one she could trust.

The leaves on the trees were just becoming yellowed, the first hints of fall had begun.

Tall evergreens stood like proud sentinels amidst the birch and poplar.

Mushrooms peaked through the bed of leaves among the trees. Some mushrooms were brown and slimy looking, others tall and frilly. Clusters grew in the deeper beds of leaves littering the forest floor.

The rosehip bushes grew thick in these parts, their fruits turning slowly from yellow to red.

Myra and Layrn walked through the forest, their footsteps loud with the crashing of fallen leaves. Myra called out for Julia.

The wolves had left. Julia, the only human being that Myra had any connection with anymore, was gone. No traces could be found on the forest floor, no hint as to where she might be. Myra was alone again.

The revelation crippled her, and she fell to her knees, sobbing. Layrn walked on. "Don't leave me Layrn!" Myra yelled after him. He had already disappeared into the brush.

"WAIT! PLEASE don't leave me alone!" but Layrn did not coming bounding around the corner.

Anger burning in her stomach she cleared her eyes of tears. Her voice shaky she called,

"Layrn! Get over here right now! That's enough."

Then, as happens when your emotions have the best of you, she laughed bitterly. That's exactly what Layrn was telling her. That's enough. You've cried over this a million times, now it was time to move on. She could feel her stomach grow hard with anger. Her wind came in hitched breaths as she stormed after him.

The term her father had used to describe when one of his daughters was furious with anger was "Spitting mad" and at that moment that was exactly what Myra was. She plowed through rosebushes ignoring brambles as they scratched at her skin. Then, she heard a rustling. Quieting her mind for a moment she listened. It was close to her.

She turned and from behind a bush stepped a sheepish looking Julia. Myra stared at her. Julia glanced up but quickly brought her eyes down to her toes.

"Hi-", she said quietly.

Myra glared.

"Hi."

Then she stormed away. Julia had to run to keep up with the older girl's long strides. "Myra, wait for me! Come back" Myra ignored her and pushed on. She could hear Julia's steps falter slightly, then, the smack of her bare feet running on the hard earth as she hurried to catch up.

"Myra, what's going on with you!?" That was it. Myra whirled

"What's going on?! I'll tell you what's going on. Since you showed up, my pack has hated me and pushed me out. One of my closest companions died and the other has disappeared and probably died too. My own dog won't even stay by my side when I need him. Oh, and I almost forgot, you ran off in a fit of childish anger and left me to pick up the mess you left. That's what's going on with me!"

Then Myra rushed off. Running deeper into the woods, not caring where her feet took her as long as it was some place where she could breathe.
Her breath was getting worse, coming in ragged gasps as she pushed herself. She could hear Julia's voice calling out to her, but she didn't bother to listen to what she said. It was Julia's fault this had happened. If Julia hadn't caused a rift in the pack, then she could have saved Traveler. Now, not only was he gone, Yiojn was probably gone for good too.
Finally, her lungs could not hold her anymore and her knees buckled. Her head was growing dizzy from the lack of air and she could feel her diaphragm spasming. She gaped like a fish with no air coming in or out. Layrn bolted out of the bushes and hit her in the side, making them both crash to the ground with the impact. Air whooshed into Myra's lungs and she panted, slowly catching her breath. Layrn untangled himself, sitting proudly beside her. Myra soon recovered. Layrn bumped against her.
Come on. Let's find Julia and get back to the pack. I have a bad feeling.
Myra blinked down at Layrn
Yes! I can talk to you with my mind. Now, come on! He sounded exasperated. Myra shook her head and followed him back through the woods.
It took them a while to get back to Julia. She was very quiet while they travelled home. Myra could still feel the anger

threatening to burst at any moment, but she held it back. It was no use fighting with the child.

Myra couldn't hear any wolf howls in the woods. The sun was setting, sending spots of brilliant sunshine among the thick evergreens.

Layrn looked at her a moment.

Why not find them this way?, he mused.

Myra controlled a shiver.

She swallowed.

"HELLO!!" She thought.

Layrn yelped, dodging away from her.

"Ouch! You don't have to yell!"

"Sorry Layrn", Myra responded quietly.

Julia seemed lost in her own world for the time being, so Myra focused on the task.

"Wolves! Where are you?"

Layrn glanced at her.

"Really? You think that randomly thinking about any old wolf out in these woods would get the response you're looking for?"

"Yeah...? Well no... I guess not."

Myra sighed; thinking a moment.

"Iko, Quiern... Where are you?"

She still felt like she had to yell inside her mind. She could see Layrn wince at the loudness.

Then, an itchy feeling clawed at the base of her skull. A deeper voice replied in her mind. She had the briefest image of Quiern flash before her eyes.

"I know you didn't bring this upon us, Wolfborn. So, I will guide you back to us.

I'm on a ridge, two leagues away, towards the setting sun. The others have gone hunting. I'm guarding the pups. Yiojn has not returned."

Myra focused again on the world before her. She hadn't noticed how quickly the sun had dropped. Only light shadows contrasted with the dark around her. She could feel a welling of hope rise within her.

"The wolves are two leagues away. They're westward of us!"

Julia looked at her, confused. They took off towards the setting sun.

Over the next few days Myra grew more accustomed to calling the wolves through her mind. Though it felt strange to her at first, she soon found she was able to contact them when they were far away from her and she could know exactly where they were. This helped with the distance between them.
Yiojn had still not returned. Myra's sorrow grew with each passing day. Julia began to help Myra with the hunting, though Myra could see how difficult it was for her. They continued to track the pack.
It had been days since Myra had found Julia. They had traveled more than five leagues without finding the wolves. Myra knew they were close however, so they pushed on deeper into the woods.
Quiern assured her that the wolves were being careful to avoid anywhere the hunters might come.

Myra was carrying Julia when they stumbled upon a cottage. Her heart rose to her throat and she quickly put Julia down. They ran for cover, staring at the cottage between the bushes. It looked well kept. A small vegetable garden sat on the southside of the building. The building itself was made of logs. A small wisp of smoke curled out of a chimney. That meant it was still inhabited! Julia pulled on Myra's arm.
"Myra, look! There's someone inside! Should we talk to them? They might be able to help us."
Julia started to step out of their cover.
Myra yanked her back.
"No! They might be in league with the king. If the king finds out that two of his sacrifices have survived, he will hunt us down and kill us! Not to mention going after Layrn and the wolves"
Myra gentled slightly,
"No. Let's watch them for a while and see who they are. We might glean some information that will help us stop the sac-

rifices"

Julia and Myra waited for a long time. Layrn had to be held between them as he continued to fuss. Eventually he slipped from their grasp. Myra, barely controlling her voice from bellowing at the dog, tried to call him back.

"Layrn! Come here boy! Come on!"

Desperate, she even yelled in her mind, *"LAYRN GET BACK HERE! You could get us all killed. Do you want to see the pack again?"*

Layrn ignored her, casually marking the trees and cottage like it was the most normal thing to do. A woman peered out at Layrn through the window. Her face was tattooed with ancient symbols. Her skin was a dark brown from the sun, and from what Myra could see through the window her hair was knotted in the way of the southern healing women.

"The woman looks like she's a healer" Myra whispered. Julia peered out of the bushes, trying to see the woman. Suddenly the door flung open, revealing the woman with a bow trained on Layrn.

She yelled,

"Get out of here! I don't want no wolves in these parts. Now get on before I shoot you dead."

Myra, without thinking, burst from the bushes.

"STOP! Don't hurt him!" she screamed.

The woman whirled, the arrow almost loosing from the string, but she managed to hold it back.

"Who are you?"

The woman's face contorted into a sneer.

"Myra. My name is Myra, I mean you no harm. Just-don't hurt my dog."

The woman leaned against the door fram, her bow still lightly trained on Myra.

"You better take care in these woods. There's wolves that would eat that pup of yours."

Myra nodded.

The woman continued

"What you doing this deep in the woods? You look like a beggar

girl. Did you get lost trying to go to the loo?" she mocked.
Myra sighed. This woman was not worth her time.
"No. I chose to come here. You just happen to live in my neck of the woods so I thought my tribe and I would scout you out" Myra said rolling her neck lazily as if she was so tough that the woman was a mere nuisance. The woman snorted,
"You and what army?"
Myra's poker face slipped for a second. Then, straightening her shoulders, she called,
"Julia, you can come out now."
Julia slipped from the bushes, also trying her hardest to give a brave face. The woman laughed
"Children! They sent children to scare me out of these woods! HAH! Like that would slow me down."
Myra sighed,
"Alright. Alright! E*nough* of this foolish banter. We're two lost souls trying to survive in this harsh wilderness. Is that so bad? Now, are you a healer woman from the southlands? Do you have herbs and training in the art of healing?"
The woman's eyebrow raised.
"Perhaps... Why do ye-ask? Is it not allowed in *your* neck a-the woods for a healer to hide away?"
Myra shifted uncomfortably,
"I want to know the ways of the healers. There are others in these woods that will need my help, but I have no knowledge of plants or the art of healing. So, I wish to learn."
The woman rocked back on her heels.
"I see... What will ye give me in return?"
Julia piped up, "We'll bring you game from our hunting. Rabbits, grouse, and the like."
Myra turned to her, meaning to shush her and tell her there was no way they could guarantee meat.
The woman intervened,
"I haven't use for others hunting meat for me. I am more than capable with a bow." She locked eyes with Myra in a glare.
"Nay, I want to learn the ways of your pretty tongue. No beggar

child would have that kind of voice from stayin' on the streets, now would they?"

Myra scrambled, surprised by the question.

"Nay, they wouldn't... I was... I was raised in a chapel, but-it burnt down and I've been on my own since then. That is, until I found Julia in the woods."

The woman brushed stray dreadlocks from her face,

"I see... Come back at sunrise and I'll see what we can do."

Then she gestured for them to go and they did, Myra calling Layrn away from the house.

The days went on. Summer slowly faded into fall.

Myra learned the ways of the healer woman. She realized now, how little she had known when Layrn had been injured. She was lucky that nothing worse had become of her while she had been in the forest this past year.

Julia learned too, and in exchange, Myra taught them the ways of the court as she knew them. Julia yearned to live in a village after Myra told them tales of her city.

The medicine woman told them that there was a good village a few miles northeast of her cottage. Julia begged and pleaded for Myra to take her there. Eventually, as winter threatened and Myra worried about the wolves,, she decided it would be best if the young girl found a proper home. Myra wouldn't be able to keep her safe in the woods, and she had no desire to live in a village so close to her father's kingdom.

So, one morning, as frost lightly covered the last remaining vegetables in the garden, Myra and Julia set out. Myra had learned from the medicine woman how to skin and tan hides. Both girls finally had proper clothes to keep them sheltered from the elements. Myra had made them warm parkas for the winter. The medicine woman had made them warm leather boots for their journey ahead. Myra would not return to the medicine woman's house after she said farewell to Julia. She planned on finding the pack again. She wanted to keep them safe from the hunters that would surely go after them again in the spring. Quiern reported that the pack was healthy, but small now that the pups had left to search out a new pack.

Myra and Julia plodded through the forest, using the mercifully brilliant sun for direction. Myra felt very lonely now. In just a few hours she would say have to say goodbye forever.

Julia seemed to pick up on Myra's trying mood and slipped her little hand into Myra's.

"Are you sure this is where you want to go?" Myra queried.

Julia looked up into her face, smiling. She still had the carefree smile of childhood. Myra longed for the time when she had been as carefree.

"I love the wolves Myra, and I'm going to miss you *terribly*." She grinned at the new word Myra had taught her.

"But, I want to have a mommy again. I don't want to hunt any more. I want to live in a house with a real fire and a warm bed."

Myra could feel tears wet her cheeks.

I want that too Julia... I want that too. She thought, as she wiped the tears from her eyes.

"But I'll come visit you!" Julia promised.

"I'm going to miss you!" Myra said, cheerfully bumping Julia's shoulder.

"You're are so brave, and cheerful and-" Myra had to take a breath to keep herself from breaking down.

"And, you are *so clever*. Don't forget that ok?"

Julia didn't seem to understand why she was so upset so she rubbed Myra's hand comfortingly with her own

"It's ok Myra, I won't forget. Everything will be alright" Myra barked a laugh, it sounded more like a sob.
"I know", she murmured wetly.
All too soon, the village came into view. Myra could sense the excitement in Julia as she was pulled by the hand, into the village.

Myra could hear dogs yapping within the village. Smoke rose from the chimneys. It seemed like a pleasant little town. The first building they came across was a tiny shrine. It was built of stone, much like a turret or castle wall might be. Yet, it was unmistakably a place of worship. Candles and incense burned within, giving it a distinct smell. The symbol of Weirion was carefully etched into the stone walls. Weirion was the God of crops and growing things. He was the father God, the King. He symbolized fertility to the land and the people. He brought either good fortune, on the house, or terrible pain. It depended on how good your standing was with him. He was the one Myra had been sacrificed to. He was the one Julia had been sacrificed to. Myra could feel the hairs rising on her neck. Her heart beat a little faster. They neared the entrance and the statue of the God peered out at them. Its stone eyes looked vacant, but stern. Myra always got shivers staring into statue eyes. There was something so real, but so incredibly wrong with statue eyes. The God was a tall muscular man. *Nothing extraordinary from any other Gods depicted in most of my kingdom's religions* she thought, producing a snort of bitter laughter from her. What *did* catch her attention was the animal skin that draped upon his shoulders. He held a spear that was driven through a startled wolf. *What was it about wolves that my culture hates so much?* This spurred a memory of what her father had said about wolves "they're beasts of the devil! Look one in the eyes and if you don't kill it your death is imminent. That's why the boys of Belloc must kill a wolf to enter manhood. They have to stare fear in the eyes and shoot it down, if they're to survive in this world." Then, he had taken the wolf skin from his shoulders, draping it around her. All she could remember was the grotesque snarl of its head and the holes where its eyes should have been. She could not remember what had happened after, but the memory of that wolf skin had given her nightmares for years.

Yet, somehow she had forgotten it. Perhaps it had been her survival instinct to shut out anything she could remember about her father. His recent appearance must have brought those memories fresh to her mind, again.

Julia tugged on her hand, prompting her to go. They left the stone shrine behind. The rest of the village was huddled close together, like newborn chicks. People stared at Myra and Julia with suspicion evident in their eyes.

Layrn bared his teeth if people stared too long. Myra could feel her heart rate accelerate, sweat began to trickle down her back. It had been so long since she had seen this many people and their hungry eyes were all too visible now. Once, she had languished in the attention she received from the common folk but now, they stared at her as if they'd like to tear her apart.

Myra took Julia to the village smithy. Myra knew that butchers, though they knew everyone, were far too suspicious of any newcomers. This was especially true for those without money. A blacksmith, however, would often be gracious and helpful to newcomers. They understood the hardships of poor families.

The clang of a hammer on iron, reverberated loudly as they came upon the smithy. The building had two walls, full of various tools. A large forge in the corner roared with a strong fire. Myra could feel the heat all the way from the entrance. A large draft horse stood tethered just inside the smithy. She could see the blacksmith breaking down the metal into a useable horseshoe with a hammer. They watched curiously for a while, until the blacksmith looked up. He grinned, waved and tucked the partially formed metal into the coals of the forge. Wiping his blackened hands on his apron, he stepped out of the loud building and into the street. "What can I do for you ladies?" He asked,

a smile painting his face. He had a close-cropped beard that was a speckled grey. His arms were large from the hard work of his trade. He had a kind round face, and, it seemed, a gentle demeanor.
"Well sir... My sister, Julia, needs a place to stay. I cannot afford to care for her any longer. I've been trapping for some of the local folk in the next town over but there's been a bit of problems there, so I had to move out. Do you know of anyone who can take a fine hardworking girl? She's like an angel, very obedient Sir. She'll keep the house clean and can even help the boys with the hunting-"
The man frowned,
"And, what about you, lass? Where are you off to?"
Myra shook her head, trying to adopt the demeanor of a peasant girl.
"I can' stay. The trappers will find me here, I can't bring that fate to my sister, Sir."
She faked a tear but suddenly could feel a whole well ready to explode at the drop of a hat.

The man crossed his arms, "I'll ask around, but you may have to stay a few days. I think Bridgit should have some space for you for a night or two if you help her in the tavern. She's towards town, big cheery building. You might hear Rupert playing his lute in there."
He studied them for a moment.
"Thank you, Sir." Myra said inclining her head.
It felt so alien to call a man Sir who did not own a title. The months that Myra had spent with the medicine woman teaching her the ways of the court, had scraped up memories and behaviors she hadn't needed for such a long time. Myra had to keep reminding herself that that was her old life. Julia clutched her hand as they traversed the town, Myra could feel the man's gaze bore into their backs. Myra felt like the earth was falling under her. She steadied herself *It's not forever Myra. You'll see her again* she soothed but she knew the words fell hollowly upon

deaf ears. Myra wouldn't be able to risk coming back for fear that someone might wonder who she was and think her a spy. There was no way she could be traced back to the throne nor be spoken of in gossip. Gossip flew like leaves on the breeze. The smaller the town the faster it would fly. Too quickly, they found the tavern. Rollicking music played inside. She could hear the laughter of men and the clang bump of platters and cups. Julia released her hand and trotted inside, excited by the joyful people within. Myra steeled herself, then stepped through the doorway.

Inside was bright with candles and a roaring fireplace. The air felt close and stuffy to Myra's sensitive nose; the smell of sweat and bodies almost made her want to vomit. She called Layrn close to her. He had followed along obediently despite his usual freedom to roam. *How lucky I am to have someone I can rely on so wholeheartedly*, she mused, her heart filling with a sad kind of love.

Julia was already at the bar, chattering away to the barman behind the counter. Myra strolled up, she could feel her shoulders and back tighten with stress. The constant twang of the lute, though pretty, was repetitive and put Myra's teeth on edge. It was all she could do to stand there and smile politely at the barman. The man broke off his conversation with Julia, Myra had missed it and wished she knew what Julia had already said.

"What can I do fer ya?" the barman spoke loudly.

To Myra's already sensitive ears, it felt like a bellow. Managing to only flinch at the intrusion she leaned forward "I'm in some trouble with the trappers, next town over. I need to scatter 'fore they find me see. But I can't take my sister with me. She doesn't deserve the life I can provide and my money's getting scarce. I was wantin' to know if there's anyone around who'd be able to take her in. She won't give you no trouble! She's an angel when it comes to manners. Will do anything at the drop of a hat."

The man's eyes narrowed, and he looked at the girl. "Whatever trouble you've been having can't be getting on this young lass's shoulders you hear? I can find someone to take her in. I can tell she'll give them no trouble, but I need to know what trouble you've been having with the trappers."

Myra swallowed. She took a deep breath. This part of the story had been planned out quickly on her trek here. She had discussed it a little with the medicine woman, Yadira, but she felt unprepared.

"There's been some rumors of some terrible beasts in these woods. Giant man-eating beasts and all that coddlewop!" The man nodded knowingly. Myra had to suppress a grin. How wonderful it was that forests like these could create all kinds of ridiculous stories. "Well…"

She leaned closer to the man and the man leaned closer to her.

"I was hunting for bear, needed some skins to sell you know" she nodded slightly, her face a perfect expression of believing the man a confidante.

"And, I came upon this monstrous beast. It was probably…"

She looked around to gauge the size, scrambling for a size that was believable but still scary.

"Probably big as the blacksmith's forge. It was covered in this long shaggy fur and had terrible eyes"

She widened her eyes and the barman's eyes widened too. She had to be careful not to push it otherwise they'd be kicked out into the street for telling tales.

"It was this giant bear. All I could think was how grand a fortune the skin would make my boss. So, I shot it with my bow, straight in the eye."

She acted out the scene of drawing back the bow and letting it fire.

"But, when my boss found out he was none too impressed. There's a story behind that bear. It was the bear of Bromen's point."

This was a common legend among the village folk, one that Gwen had told her about when she was very young. "And, if you killed it, you cursed anyone who used it's skin." Then she straightened, growing serious.

"But, I don't believe that coddlewop! It was just a large bear. One that would have made me fortunes, alas my boss did not let me have it back and he's sent some of his men after me. So, I must hide from them and not show up here for a long time."

The barman leaned back, grabbing a glass from the table and polishing it with a rag. He seemed to ponder her story for a while. She hoped desperately that she hadn't over embellished the story.

"We'll take her… But promise you don't bring any of this trouble upon her head."

Myra bowed her head in sincerity, "I promise on my life."

Julia looked between them, trying to understand the kind of half-spoken agreement that passed between them.

"Bridgit!" The barman yelled behind him and a short plump woman came out. Her arms were large from carrying platters of food and drink for a living. Her face was ruddy and hard, but Myra could tell that behind the hard exterior was a kind woman.

"My wife, this young girl" he pointed to Julia "needs a safe place to live. I've offered for her to stay here in exchange for her help in the tavern. Her sister is in deep trouble and can't keep her but the trouble I think will stay with her and not be left with the little one."

Bridgit looked from the barman to Myra and then to Julia.

Julia stared at her with big eyes, she clasped onto Myra's hand tightly.

Bridgit bent down, her knees crackling. "Hello there! What's your name?" Julia looked up to Myra who nodded her chin at the woman "go ahead" Myra said encouragingly

"My name's Julia." Julia said, her voice quiet.

"That's a beautiful name! Now let's show you around the place and find you a good place to sleep. You can help me first in cleaning the rooms. I think your little arms are strong enough to hold a broom, don't you think?"

Julia nodded vigorously. She let go of Myra's hand and clasped the woman's hand. They walked off down the hall. Julia turned around, her hand still clasped in the woman's hand and gave a little wave, a lopsided grin painting her face. Myra held back a surge of tears as she watched the little girl skip off behind the woman, happy as a clam. Layrn tried to follow her but Myra called him back. Swiping away a tear she turned back to the barman "Thank you! I'll never forget this kindness."

The man nodded; his face full of pity "I'm sorry you'll have to leave her behind. She seems like a nice girl"

Myra swallowed back more tears "She's the best kid I've ever met... You take care of her now!" She said seriously, then before he could answer she called Layrn and ran out of the tavern.

Dream

The winter storm had passed. Leaving drifts of snow and cracked trees in its wake. The wolves had hunkered down the night before the storm, warning Myra of the danger coming. Myra had been away from her cottage, hunting, when she heard them. The wind had risen, gusting fine snow into Myra's eyes. Her weathered face barely noticed the cold as the snow brushed across her skin. For thirty years Myra had weathered through the winter in these woods. For a time, she had lived in a village with Layrn, but the constant noise and thrum of the people had driven her crazy.

It had been thirty-eight years since Layrn had passed from the world.

She'd given up trying to live among people. The wolves were her only family; the forest her home. Hoisting the grouse higher over her shoulder, Myra ploughed through the snow. It was a good life. She'd saved many children in her time. The wolves were no longer hunted, and the pack had grown over time. Now more than twelve wolves made up the pack. As Myra crested a hill, she saw them. A sleek black female Myra called Ishna was the Alpha now. A distant granddaughter of Echo and Traveler. The newest member of the pack was a white female. She was a tiny thing, most likely malnourished as a pup. Yet her eyes held the same spirit and knowing as Yiojn had. Myra's heart ached at the memory of the white wolf. No closure had come for Myra with Yiojn. The wolf had never returned after Traveler was killed and a part of Myra had always wished that she would return.

The white wolf loped up to Myra, tail wagging in greeting. The other wolves barked excitedly, dancing around Myra. They spun around happily; Myra's heartbeat grew stronger with the love of these creatures. *You are all I need, dear ones.* Myra thought lovingly to them.

That night as the wind whistled angrily at the door, Myra and the wolves curled up before the fire. Lulled by the lazy flames before them, they soon fell asleep.

That night, Myra dreamt of her first winter in the forest. She could see Traveler coming to her with the deer haunch in his mouth. Except, instead of the deer haunch that had saved her, it was a child. A dead child. Myra recoiled.

"Why are you bringing this to me, Traveler? Have you no respect for the child whose life has been lost?" She asked him. Yiojn appeared at her hip and looked up at her,

"You must stop this cruelty Myra; you must return to your kin and stop them. Too many souls cannot find peace in these woods."

Myra could feel herself quaking, shivering in fear. She looked down at the child's body and saw it was Julia. The young girl suddenly opened her eyes and reached out for Myra "Myra! Myra you must stop this! You must stop the sacrifices!" she screeched.

Myra woke with a start, breathing heavily she clung to the bed, trying to reassure herself that it was all a bad dream.

"Just a dream" she breathed. She looked to the sleeping wolves and saw the white wolf staring at her, those same golden eyes baring into hers.

"You must return to your kin and stop them", the wolf said in her mind. Myra burst into tears.

"I can't- I can't go back there!", she said, feeling her breath hitching in her throat. "I-I can't face them"

Trust

"Do you trust her?" Tico stared into Liana's face. The old Queen closed her eyes, composing herself.

"Yes, I trust her. She said herself that she could have created an entire army from those she saved yet she didn't."

"Or so she says," Tico played idly with the rings on his fingers, rolling them back and forth.

"We're lucky she didn't, otherwise we would have been overrun by rebels and the monarchy would be destroyed by now."

Liana looked away irritated by the conversation

"Don't remind *me* how close we are to being torn down by the people." She walked to the window and stared out at the lush garden below. Myra was lounging on the lawn, her dogs surrounding her in a contented bundle. Liana whispered quietly to herself,

"Why did you come Myra?" *Why did you come back? You could have lived your life in freedom, instead you risk taking over the throne and never being able to go back to the forest and your hounds.*

Liana could feel the familiar sorrow building within her. She would rule until her dying breath and could never experience the freedom of expression she had been allowed in her childhood.

Tico stepped close to her and she heard the sharp inhale of a guard by the door.

"Mother, let us not fret over this woman. She may go quietly back to her woods and leave us in peace."

"She never. Leaves. *Quietly*." Liana stated then stormed out of her chambers, guards scurrying behind her.

Liana had to find some air, had to breathe, where people weren't breathing down her neck, or watching her every movement. She rushed to the roof of the palace, where only her guards would follow.

Climbing up the stairs she could hear her breath coming in gasps, but she couldn't falter. She needed this. Throwing open the door to the level palace roof she stepped out. There were low walls all around her, notched to allow bows and cannons to fire through. The wind whipped at Liana's hair, catching her breath in its ferocity.

Here, was where she felt safe. She could see the whole of Belloc before her, tiny cottages crammed together, with the hulking mass of the castle walls surrounding them.

Below she could see Myra, still sprawled comfortably in the palace gardens. The gardens were situated on the outskirts of the palace. The stables were beyond them, so that when you sat beneath the lilac trees, you could hear the nickers of the horses and their galloping hooves as they frolicked in the paddocks.

The courtyard in the middle of the palace held a grand fountain, the goddess of the moon spewing water from her hands in offering to the sky.

"Surrounded by walls. Always surrounded by walls" Liana murmured.

She had always thought that she would have the power to change things when she became queen. What twenty years on the throne had taught Liana was that she was merely a puppet with a voice. She could say whatever she wanted but without her people's agreement she had no power to make that change.

Now Myra was back. *She was alive!* Liana had assumed that Myra had died within the first year. They'd known that survival was slim in those woods.

Liana and her sisters had made a pact to try to give Myra the fighting chance in surviving, but they knew that the woods were a harsh place.

Liana had vowed to herself the day that Myra had been sacrificed that she would stop it. She would stop the sacrifices from ever happening again. But she'd been bullied into submission by her councilors. Micareon had been the only one she could trust but he went so closely by the book that she was basically defenseless in her argument to stop the sacrifices. She'd given up hope long ago, had let her strong backbone fall and allowed the councilors to take over. She still held her title, still sat upon the throne but she felt like a puppet being played at a theatre, unknowingly playing along with someone else's script.

Now Myra was back, and she changed all that. Myra had done the impossible; she had survived. When their sisters had died from the mere touch of a wolfskin, Myra had lived amongst the beasts, traversed countless miles of forest and had come home unscathed. The woman was remarkable! Liana's old hope returned, prickling quietly at her stomach, reminding her of the butterflies that used to flutter within, when hope rose within her. She hadn't had hope for such a long time.

Maybe there was a chance for her to reconcile with Myra. Maybe she would be able to stop the sacrifices.

Liana had duties in the court so Tico decided it was time to show his aunt who was truly in charge.

He sauntered into the garden, disgusted by the strong perfume of the roses his mother loved so dearly. Myra lay sprawled on her back, face up to the sky, appearing to all the world as though she was napping. The dogs eyed him suspiciously and grumbled a warning. With lightning speed that made Tico flinch she was on her feet. She stared at him; eyes hard with distrust. "What brings you, my Prince?" she asks warily.

"I come in peace, dear Aunt."
He lifts his palms towards her to show that he has nothing to hide.
"I've only come to hear the tale of how you came to us." She snorted.
"Like hell you are!"
With a low whistle to the dogs, she padded off towards the courtyard.

Tico followed, anger wanting to overtake him,

"Lady Myra! You cannot address me in that way" Myra looked over her shoulder, her gaze could have shot daggers.

"What is it you really want to know? Get to the chase or be off with you. I've no time to speak in tongues." Tico bristled but kept his voice a deadly calm.

"How many people did you save?"

Myra turned to face him; her weathered features taut with anger.

"Fifty-three... I saved fifty-three women from the fate that was left to them. Only a few survived... The woods are a terrible place sometimes." She gazed into nothingness between them, her eyes looked melancholy.

"Where did the ones who survived go?"

She shook her head.

"I can't answer that, for I only gave them the tools to survive. Some went into the nearby villages and lived quiet lives there. Others became rebels and fought to stop the sacrifices. Most of those women, though far braver than I, died a terrible death."

She shook tears from her eyes. *What a terribly weak woman*, Tico thought.

"You know how many dead that I found whilst I lived in those woods? Do you have any inkling!?" Her voice was a barely controlled yell. Tico watched her, not buying into her sob story.

"Hundreds! *Hundreds* of children, some only newborns. Some died in the frosts of winter. Their bodies would be rock hard from the cold, their tiny eyelashes covered peacefully in frost" she swallowed

"Others would be rotting in the heat of summer... I remember them all, Tico. Each tiny face. Knowing that my lack of courage caused them this suffering... That's why I came back." She pushed past him towards the garden again.

"I tried to scare the hunters off. I tried to keep the sacrifices from happening." She trailed off, Tico followed her as she went to a large willow, her hand grasping at its bark like a lifeline.

"I created stories of terrible beasts that lurked in the forest and ambushed hunts as they went after my wolves... they hunted them *only* for the sake of their honor..."

She stared at the bark, then violently slammed her fist into its rough surface. When it came away her knuckles were bleeding. Tico backed away a couple steps, perturbed. She whirled on him; her eyes feral with anger.

"I was the evil witch they said lurked in the forest. I would get them all turned around in that forest and make it so they would never wish to come back again.
I would steal their horses and distort their minds with mild poison that would wear off by the time they came back to their villages. But it didn't stop the sacrifices, just made it *worse*.
They thought if they killed their daughters in the light of the full moon that they might appease me. They slit their throats, Tico. They killed them. In the name of a God that does not exist."
She crumpled, hard, onto her knees. The dogs surrounded her. One stared Tico down and walked towards him making the

Prince dance away in fear.

"Control your dogs!" Myra laughed bitterly

"You think these are dogs! Hah! Look closely at the wolves your family call demons." Tico backed up more, calling to his guards. They surrounded him but even they danced away from the wolf. Myra lifted her head, "Come, Amoux. There's no point in chasing these ones." The wolf trotted back to her. A wayward guard started to unsheathe his sword, Tico laid a hand on the man "Don't." he said, and they left.

Yiojn had spent five, long, hungry days outside the city. She had plotted ways of tracing the men back to their leader. There were too many stray dogs in the city, that would fight her just for the sport of it. It wouldn't be worth her while to get there.

Traveler's death still held over her, darkly.

She missed the pack. It felt so isolated on the edge of the forest. She could no longer hear the distant howls of the wolves, so she knew she was far. A wolf's howl could cover up to a league away in the forest and three leagues on open ground. At night the forest was quiet. Owls sometimes passed through, but it wasn't nearly as alive as the rest of the forest. She often heard the mournful howls that the dogs within the city made. They could never replace the pure howls of the wolves though.

It was tonight that she pondered why she had come. She had been ignoring this growing feeling of helplessness for days now. She had known when she set out that the journey would be futile but something about it had seemed to ring with purpose.

Yiojn could feel the tingle in her mind that was the sign that visions were about to come to her.
She lay down preparing for the worst but hoping for an answer to this dilemma.

Before her eyes danced the fleeting image of a mangy dog. She could see from its haggard appearance and foaming mouth that it was infested with rabies. She shied away from it despite it being only an image. It spoke, its voice gurgling with fluid.

"To stop the killings you must sacrifice. Poison the king with your fur and he will stop the killings. But you must be discrete lest he suspect disease within the pack and threatens to kill them all! You will not live to discover the effects of your journey... Though it will spread further than you ever intended. Beware what you wish." Then the dog before her, hacked up the fluids and howled, the terrible sound was like it was drowning.
She wanted to turn away, but she had to watch as the dog before her gurgled, choked and fell dead to the ground.
Then the vision was gone. Before her lay only the forest, no dogs lay before her and no spittle soaked into the ground. She licked her chops.
"I'm going to die aren't I, Traveler?", she thought numbly. She looked out to the wastelands she had traversed behind the men. The tree stumps created strange shadows on the ground while the moon above shined a pale grey, almost full and so bright but something looked wrong with it. A twitch ran up Yiojn's spine. Something ominous was going to happen tomorrow.

Morning came dark and stormy. The wastelands to the left of the city looked like gravestone sentinels in the morning light. Yiojn had decided what the plan was going to be. Her only way of killing the king was if her coat, as the spirit had prophesized, were poisoned. The only way her fur could have poison on it that would kill him would be if she was diseased and the disease spread to him. That was what she had understood from the spirit's look and what they had said.

She whined. It was not a light decision for her to decide to end her days in this way and at this time. She took off into the forest. One disease she knew would spread to a human was common in these woods. She'd seen it before. Especially near the city.

She stalked many animals, searching for the one that would feed her but ultimately kill her. A lone coyote, mangy and scrambling to get up was the one that she found. *How lucky... I've found an advanced victim of the disease.* she said sarcastically in her mind.

She hid and the thought of how she would make it to the king puzzled at her. Her white coat was considered precious among the humans, or so her dam had told her. Her grand dam had been a white wolf and was also a seer.

She had warned Yiojn of the risks her white coat would place her in. Her tail wagged. Kill this coyote, contract the disease but get killed before it was obvious, then she would be brought to their alpha on a golden platter.

It was risky though.

She could die before the men found her, or she could be killed, and her skin sold off. She had a surety though - the spirits had told her that it would happen. She just had to trust.

She leapt on the coyote, pinning it to the ground. It snarled at her, going berserk. She felt the bite on her foreleg before she saw it.

Pain ripped up along her body and she killed it with a quick snap of her jaws. She pulled back, staring down at her leg. A large bite mark oozed with blood. She licked it.

I'm done for now. Her mind stated simply, the thought sounding ironic to her own ears.

I'm sorry Wolfborn, you will have to guard the pack. I have followed my fate, but I did not expect it to take me this way. Then she walked off, sickened by the state of the coyote. She could not eat her relative, no matter how hungry she was. She came upon an old scavenged carcass. It still had some meat on it that would fill her belly. So, she feasted, chasing off turkey vultures that threatened to steal her meal. When she was full, she paid her respects to the animal and left. Yiojn's leg throbbed but the bleeding had stopped. She would have to wait a while. She would draw the hunters in but give herself enough time for the effects of the disease to set in.

Just enough time to say goodbye and enjoy the warm sun on my fur and the last joys of the fall.

She slept for some time dreaming of the pack. Echo stood alone in the forest, she seemed to know it was Yiojn who saw her, and she called to her, "come home". Yiojn tried to rush to her, tried to find comfort in Echo's voice. "I can't!" she cried, trapped in place by some invisible force "forgive me". She saw the hurt in her dam's eyes and then she woke with a start. A low throb still emanated from her leg. It was red, blood still crusted on the wound, but she didn't smell infection. The dream rushed back to her. "Echo" her mind rolled the word around in her head and she could feel the familiar sorrow resting in her gut. She would never see her dam again. Nor her littermates; Iko and Quiern. *The big blundering oafs* she thought fondly.

Myra wandered into the palace, her talk with Tico still fresh in her mind. A page boy rushed up to her, he bowed.

"The Queen wishes for you to join her for luncheon, Lady Myra. In her chambers.... She wishes a private audience with you. Shall I give her your reply?"

Myra smiled sadly. It felt wrong to be waited on like this, the boy could have so many more things he could do with this short life they were each given. She shook herself

"No, I shall come and tell her myself... Thank you." The boy bowed and trotted off in the other direction. Myra found Liana's chambers with little confusion, it was good that the guards assigned her were so knowledgeable of the palace.

The guards posted outside of Liana's doors bowed courteously and bid her entry. Inside was an extravagant display of wealth. The study was large, with big, plush chairs arranged around a wide marble-stone fireplace. On the walls hung extraordinarily detailed tapestries, depicting great victories. One was covered in smaller scenes each depicting a popular legend of the land. Myra saw the bear of Bromen's point and smiled.

That was how it all began. She wanted to laugh and weep at the memory. She could still remember the feel of Julia's soft little hand letting go of hers as she followed the innkeeper's wife, her gaze only briefly looking back at Myra to give a quick smile and a wave. Then she had disappeared up the staircase and that had been the last Myra had ever seen of her.

A servant stepped in,

"Queen Liana will be only a moment, Lady Myra. She's just finishing her bath."

Myra inclined her head "No rush."

She smiled at the woman, and the woman smiled back at her genuinely, then lowered her eyes, abashed at having stared at a noblewoman. As the servant rushed out of the room Liana entered. She wore an elegant gown, it was a turquoise shade of blue, and in a simple cut. It made Liana look years younger, her white hair was piled elegantly on her head, her crown highlighting the look. Myra stared at her, stunned. Liana laughed uncomfortably and sat close to the fire; the flames crackled peacefully.

"I don't think you were even this beautiful when we were girls!" Myra grinned.

Liana rolled her eyes.

"Do sit down, and stop gaping like a fool! We're far too old to look this becoming." She ran a hand over her face in mock disgust. Myra laughed and sat down.

"What was it that you wished to talk to me about, Liana?" Liana again ran a hand over her face.

"I wanted to explain to you how Gwen, Ariea, Frieda and… Our father died. I think it's important that you know."

Myra looked into the flames.

"Oh"

Liana settled more comfortably then called one of her servants over, they came with a platter of cold cheeses and fresh bread.

"Thank you, that will be all. Make sure the others go out with you."

The serving woman inclined her head and left.

"Well this is a pleasant way to enjoy luncheon" Myra bared her teeth but it wasn't a smile.

Liana waved a hand of dismissal,

"You need to know this."

Myra crossed her arms, leaning back into the chair.

"Go on then."

"They died from…" Liana clears her throat, shifting in her chair.

"From a wolf."

Myra sits up,

"A wolf?!"

Liana nods.

"Yes, the wolf was infested with the plague. It was in the very early stages, so we didn't catch it until Gwen began having symptoms after being the third of the royal family to hold the wolf skin"

Liana wiped her nose,

"Father was first to go. Then Ariea and Frieda died within days of each other… They'd always been close. Gwen was the last to go. The last thing I remember her saying was that she hoped that you-" she looks into Myra's eyes,

"-found peace with the wolves. I'd always shaken it off as some maddened words from a dying woman. I see now that she knew far more of your fate then the rest of us"

Myra could feel her throat clenching, but she felt separated from her body as if she were looking down on herself.

"Was the wolfskin black?", she asked, staring into the flames.

Liana could tell that Myra was hundreds of leagues away at that moment; lost in her grief.

"No." she paused "It was white"

Myra sobbed abruptly and crumpled.

"Yiojn!", she cried. "Oh, *Gods*! Yiojn!"

She began to shiver in shock. Liana called for her servants, yelling for a doctor.

A while later after the doctor had seen to Myra and she lay on Liana's bed, the Queen entered. Myra looked drawn, her eyes slightly bloodshot and her face pale. Liana called Myra's dogs in and they rushed up to Myra, a couple clambered onto the bed and lay beside her. Myra smiled, petting each furry head.

"Are these wolves?" Liana asked cautiously. Myra scanned the room and seeing no one present, nodded.

Liana let out a deep sigh.

"We can't let anyone know that they are. Otherwise they'll be killed"

Myra nodded.

"Liana, tell me, how did they get a white wolfskin?"

Liana sat gingerly on the edge of the bed, keeping as far from the wolves as possible.

"There was a white wolf hanging around the outskirts of the city. It was being a nuisance, killing livestock and behaving quite erratically... That should have been one of our first clues", she mused.

"The farmers threatened to kill it and make a rug of it. But father... He always liked unusual, expensive things. So, he took the nobles out for a hunt. The wolf was easy to kill having nowhere to hide amidst the wastelands. He took it to be made into a wolfskin cloak. He thought it would bring him great power. Alas, that power killed him." Liana sighed, seeming more regretful than sad.

"It stopped the wolf hunting though. That made Gwen happy. She always believed you and Layrn would have come back as wolves in your next life."

Myra stared at the ceiling.

"The wolf's name was Yiojn. She was a powerful creature, full of magic."

She slammed her fist on the bed.

"If the fool hadn't killed Traveler, our sisters would have been spared.", she said harshly.

Liana cocked her head "who was Traveler?"

Myra shook her head, lost for words with emotion.

"He was the one who saved me my first winter in the woods. Without him I would have died. He was the most loyal, brave, and compassionate wolf I have ever met." She sighed shakily.

"Baird killed him to reach his rite of passage into manhood."

Myra's lip trembled. She closed her eyes, composing herself.

"Oh"

Liana was surprised by her sister's grief. There was so little she knew about Myra now. It had been too long since they had known each other. Now it was like meeting a new person and them only telling fragments of their past.

Wavering

Tico paced inside his rooms, his hands absently fiddling with his dagger. It had a handle made of brass and was polished till it gleamed. It was a double-edged dagger. The edges were sharpened to a razor point. Tico loved to twist it over in his hands, careful not to cut himself. There was something comforting and powerful when he held it in his grip.

How was he supposed to get the throne if his aunt threatened his position?

The Queen was setting him up to never be on the throne. He still hadn't married, no fault of his own. She had simply never loved him like Suzanne. He'd been the second best, the afterthought. His father had never spent time with them. *Got himself killed in a crusade by a lowly peasant who had tricked him into thinking that he was innocent and unarmed. Father had been a weak man. Too soft in the heart to others and yet not soft enough with him.* He had tried to train Tico's arrogant confidence out of him, but it only made the anger grow stronger.

He was still pacing when a page boy trotted in, out of breath.

"Prince Tico... The... The Queen would like an immediate audience with you."

Tico gestured the boy away and his servants hastily prepared him for the Queen.

Sauntering down the hallway, he stared lazily at the subjects who passed him, their eyes full of questions.

"I'm here, your Majesty." Tico bowed mockingly, one of the younger women subjects suppressed a giggle. The Queen sat stonily on her throne, her manner foreboding. Tico could tell she was angry. He straightened.

"I called you here because it has come to my attention that you interrogated Lady Myra. This was out of line. I also noticed that she was injured from the exchange. Do you care to explain yourself?" A quiet gasp blew up among the subjects.

Tico felt humiliated. *How dare she word it like that!*

"I did not *interrogate* her. I simply asked how she came to be here and asked further into it so I might understand why she would come back. As for her injury that was self-inflicted. She threw her fist into a tree."

A snort erupted from one of the subjects.

Tico's face grew hot.

"The Weasel has forced the story this way, so my mother may have all the power!", his mind hissed.

"I see... And why would Lady Myra *punch* a tree? Was she aiming violence at you and *missed*?"

Tico started to stride forward, but the Queen put up a hand.

"Peace, my Prince. I do not mean to ridicule you; I only wish to understand"

Tico wanted to spit at her.

"Oh really?! You don't wish *to ridicule* me? You've changed the story around so that *I* am the one at fault here. That woman is a raving lunatic! She's spent far too long in those woods. She punched the tree because she was so angry at not being able to *save* all the sacrifices. I'm *surprised* the Gods haven't shot her down with lightning by now for that treachery!"

The Queen stood, her normally composed features set in a snarl of rage.

"DO NOT speak of her as such! If you have opinions of Lady Myra, I wish you keep them to yourself. I did not ask you to speculate about the God's hand in this. Now, did Lady Myra aim violence towards you or not?"

A little voice inside Tico said *say she did! Say she aimed to hit you in a fit of madness and that she only missed because you ducked.*

Tico said quietly, looking at his feet

"She did, your Majesty." The Queen sat back stunned.

"I see... What did you say before she tried to punch you?"
"I said that she- "

Myra burst into the throne room; the wooden beads woven into her hair clinking together like wind chimes as she stormed in. Her face was flushed with anger and her brows were knit tightly together. Not forgetting her position, she bowed to the Queen and in the same fluid motion stepping up and closer to her sister. The Queen was still on her throne. Tico stood before her, his eyes darting between Myra and his mother, trying to determine where the verbal blow would come from next.
Myra stepped equally in line with Tico.
"I demand that you change the law forcing the sacrifices!" she announced, slightly breathless.
A moment later Myra's guards rushed in, their armor clanging noisily. They bowed, murmuring apologies through large gasps of air. Liana's gaze returned to Myra.
"What is your case against this law?" she said loudly, projecting her sovereignty. Myra looked just about ready to scream at her in frustration, but she composed herself, barely.
"You may not be aware of this, seeing as you have not spent the amount of time as I have in the forbidden forest. When children are sacrificed, they are left with only the clothes on their back. They are expected to die peacefully and appease the Gods... What a joke that is" Myra snorted, disgusted by the idea.
"Those girls are not killed quickly by blade or predator but instead are left to die the death of famine. You do not realize how many children have been sacrificed in my time." She said this with pity instead of a demeaning tone. She closed her eyes, flinching at memories that played behind them.
"Hundreds died in that wood. All nameless, placeless, starved... corpses." Her breath hitched.
"The Gods do not take them. I saw more than my share of their ghosts. Though who would believe a *raving* lunatic"

Myra stared pointedly at Tico.

"I wish the law to be changed so these children do not have to suffer as I have. No one deserves this fate, no matter what gender or race they were born into. So, I plead to you, dear sister, have mercy on them as you have with me."

Liana sat stonily on the throne.

"I should have had you executed when you returned. That is what the law demands should any of the sacrifices return. I spared you even though it goes against my better judgement."

Myra felt the impact of her words like a blow.

"You have caused only disturbance in my court since you arrived. I did not wish for you to return so that you could play on my conscience and make me question my duty. The people will not accept a change in this law so lightly. Times have been hard, and crops are low. If I were to change this law, there would be an uproar. We already have enough pressure from our borders that to have inner turmoil in the kingdom would be fatal to us all."

Myra's hands are clenched at her sides.

"I see... I see where you stand, your Majesty."

She bows tightly.

"I will not be back again."

Turning on her heel, Myra storms out, slamming the giant throne room doors behind her with a loud bang.

The Queen stood and looked to Tico.

"We will meet here again tomorrow, and you may complete your story. For now, I need to rest, it has been a trying day. Please see to our subjects, Prince Tico. I thank you." Then the Queen left, her guards and servants in toe.

Tico sat on his lesser throne, staring at his mother's elegantly carved one with envy. He nodded for the guard to start allowing the subjects in.

Myra ran to her chambers and threw open the wardrobe. Inside were elegant dresses of different attractive colors. On the bottom lay a discarded pile of her old clothes. She pulled them out. Laying out the clothes before her she took account of anything missing. Soft deerskin breeches, some worn wool lined leather boots that Yadira, the medicine woman had given her. She unfolded a green linen tunic, embroidered with the symbol of a wolf, given to her by a gypsy family she had saved who had gotten lost in the woods after being hunted by the kingdom. She draped the last article of clothing on the bed, a long thick-fur cloak made from the skin of a bear.

Changing, she withdrew a pendant from the pocket of her breeches. It was a canine tooth from a dog, carved in the image of a wolf howling. Draping it over her neck she walked out. Her guards followed her, nervous of what she was doing. She wound her way through the many hallways, her head held high. She finally made it to the gardens, where the wolves greeted her. She shouldn't have brought them here. They were nervous and hadn't eaten much in the past few days. With a gentle grunt she called the wolves and they stepped out into the streets of the city. Her guards clambered to keep up with her long strides, they shied from the wolves at her feet. From the corner of her eye she could see one split off and return to the castle. *An informant for my sister. How fitting! Now she'll probably have me hung for leaving without permission. Well bully for her, I know the forest better than anyone.* She swept out the front gates, the guards of the gate called to her to not stray to the forest, it was forbidden. She laughed.

"Oh, I won't be back so don't worry about that!", she called. Her guards finally stopped her at the tree line. "Lady Myra! Stop!"

She turned, growing impatient of the constant people around her who moved so slowly.

"I understand that you have strict orders to bring me back to the Queen. I'm afraid I won't be able to do that. I also know that your protection stops at this point. Don't worry I can take care of myself. I don't suppose I'll be seeing you again."

She nodded to them and stepped into the forest. It felt like crossing a threshold to another world where she would never come in contact with this nightmare of a city again. She sighed. It felt good to be home. The wolves, released of their agreed upon duties bounded before her, happy to be free of the constraints and noise of the city.

They returned to her small cabin. It was only big enough for a bed and a fireplace. It was well insulated against the cold but roughly built and dark. It hunkered close to a hillside where a small den resided. The wolves gathered around the den gratefully.

Myra opened the door to her little cabin, arms laden with branches she had stacked at the doorway.

Lighting a fire in the stone fireplace, she sat, pondering the last few days. Part of her mind said. *There. it's done. The sacrifices will stop in time and we won't ever have to go back to that retched place again.* In her heart of hearts she knew that she had made a mistake, letting her anger override and insulting those people. It was so hard though, with those painful memories scraping up her insides and reopening old wounds. It didn't matter how long she worked to heal those wounds they still were barely kept from festering. It didn't help that her sister had told her that she would rather her dead than before her. That was the hardest sword to swallow. She cried. It was better to cry than to hold that anger and hurt inside. It was something that she could do to soothe herself for a while, but she knew she would have to return. The deed was not done. The ghosts that burdened her would not leave if she did not stop the suffering.

After a while, she gathered herself and went out into the woods in search of food. Fall was a good time for her. Trees let go of many of their limbs, allowing her to gather their wood for fire. Mushrooms were abundant, as were the rose hips and pine nuts. It would be slim pickings today, since she hadn't much sunlight left. The wolves lounged luxuriously on the sun warmed earth. Myra could feel a tension lifting from her shoulders as she gathered food for her meal. The tight quarters of the city had stifled her, there was no room for her legs to stretch out in the long strides she was accustomed to. The dresses, though beautiful and soft, constrained her and made her feel like she was gasping for air.

Out here the air was fresh, the forest quiet, and her legs had endless miles they could wander. Myra smiled. *I should have been a poet. I could think of endless words to describe the beauty of a forest yet never find a word to speak in conversation with another human.* Myra's mind tried to skirt around the fact that she would have to return to the city, to the humans. Words would be the only way she would be able to change the fate of her people. Yet the thought still passed her mind, skittering like a startled mouse. *I must convince the people, before I can convince the court.*

She returned to her cabin and forced herself to relish in the experience, in case it was her last of the place.

A week passed before Myra finally mustered the will to return, knowing that her eyes would never again grace those of her pack. The distant grandchildren of Echo and Layrn. She could still see the resemblance of her beloved dog within them. The way they cocked their heads. Their doggy grins and soft eyes.

Yet they still held much of Echo's charisma and mystery. She could not understand them fully as she had with Layrn, but that was the excitement of it. She would never know what the wolves might do next. Myra gazed at the cabin.

She'd built it so long ago, full of hope and wonder at where the years might lead her. So many memories.

Linking minds with those of the pack she said *"I must go now. Do not follow me, the path I lead is not for you to follow. Be strong my pack, May the moon guide your way. I love you"*

Then with only the clothes on her back she turned to the city, it's high stone walls foreboding in the mist of the early morning. *Goodbye, forest that has cared for me so long. I will miss your quiet murmurings and joyful birdsong.*

Story Told

Myra stood at the entrance to the city of Belloc. Its gate towered above her, stone slick with morning mist. The portcullis bared its teeth above the entrance in an angry snarl. Guards stood out on the walls like the spikes of a porcupine. People entered and exited the city in throngs. Donkeys, with carts full of merchandise lugged along the road, while wealthy mercenaries rode out on nimble, palfrey horses, built for the speed of travel. Pages followed behind, leading the knights' battle horses.

Gwen had once told Myra a story of a page boy who worked for a knight, but the knight was a woman and they fell in love. The page boy became the knight's protector against wayward mercenaries and bandits on the road. Myra had loved that story, and they had often speculated what knights could secretly be women and their pages, their lovers.

A slow smile crept over Myra's face. Her sister lived on through her stories.

Today she would have to take Gwen's role as storyteller. It was today that she would change the course of her country's history. Myra followed an alley into a busy square; arrested by a large statue portraying the statue of King Belloc killing a demonic looking wolf with a spear. *How fitting*, Myra thought sarcastically. Drawing on the skills she had learned as a child of commanding a grand audience, she stepped onto the pedestal of the statue.

"People of Belloc! What I have to say is important to your daughters' survival." She announced, feeling self-conscious as people began to stop, some waved her off dismissively.

"The sacrifices do not appease the Gods! In fact, the Gods do not

accept the offerings!"
Some people stood in front of her, arms crossed.
Myra swallowed. It had been so long since this many people had stood before her. So long since she had taken this role.
"I was sacrificed as a young girl and *I* have seen firsthand the pain and suffering those you abandon must suffer... They die the death of famine; the worst death you could bestow upon a person. Your daughters are innocent, they have done no wrong... We cannot change the gender with which we were born with, though I know many who would have chosen otherwise if they had had the chance."
The people watched, hooked by her telling, but still not trusting her story.
"The Gods did not take me."
Someone shouted that it was because she was a demon and no God would take a demon. Ruffled, Myra continued, her voice growing in anger and defense. She had to convince these people that this was no longer acceptable.
"They left hundreds of children to *die*. They died in the freezing cold, with no warmth, no food, and no shelter. The Gods do not want your daughters!", she yelled, years of anger and frustration pushed into those few words.
More softly she said,
"They do not judge as we do, the misfortune of another daughter. The Gods wish us to be at peace with who we are!"
People scoffed and went off on their way.
"Would you want your children to suffer?", she shouted angrily at their retreating backs
"Did you want them to die slow, painful deaths so you may clear your conscience of them? How *dare* you back down from your duty as parents to protect them!"
Some people turned and stormed back to her and Myra immediately regretted angering them. She wasn't under the Queens' protection anymore and could easily be killed. Then a funny thought occurred to her.
Isn't it ironic that I should fear my own kind more than the wild

wolves and the forest? She straightened, projecting a confidence she didn't have right now.

"How dare you insult us! We took care of them as long as we could, but we need boys for our families to survive in these parts. We did the only thing we could for the good of all!", a man shouted.

Myra's inner voice scoffed, *of course! This man hadn't had the kind of connection that parents are supposed to have with their children, he just thought of them as a survival tool.*

Others joined the throng now, chanting

"Demon!" and "Witch!"

telling her that she was a mad woman and had no right to be there.

She tried to argue but, the throng was too loud and too big.

She had to retreat. Climbing off the pedestal of her father's statue she lost her balance for a moment and clung to the statue. Looking at it's cold surface in surprise she found that she had grabbed its hand. She withdrew as if she had been stung.

"It's just a statue", she breathed, as she rushed out of the square and into a quieter part of the city.

Myra would have to find a quieter way to educate the people - something that wouldn't get them as riled up. She thought about Gwen, trying to conjure up long ago memories of her sister's superb storytelling skills.

Nothing.

Gwen had had the knack that Myra would never have.

Myra had told stories in her time at court, and even to the people she had saved but now when she needed it, her words failed her.

What was there she could say? What had happened was not easy to tell. She remembered one of her teachers explaining how rumors spread, a lifetime ago when she was still a Princess.

"You only have to tell one person if you tell the right one. They will do the rest of the work for you. The rumors that spread the quickest are the ones regarding leaders... So be careful what you say to anyone." The words rung inside her head.

She strolled aimlessly, no longer chased by anyone and with nowhere to go.

The streets were narrow, full of large buildings that rose up into the sky. Barely any dirt here, she thought sadly. The only dirt was the terrible grime of cities. Like a static dust, it would gather on you and stick, leaving you covered in it.

Myra's body grew weary, the hard cobblestones below her killed her feet beneath her soft leather shoes.

She found an inn; the interior was warm and inviting. Above her a sign creaked, it read "The Wild Goose Inn" the sign depicted a painted goose flying high in the sky, a cheerful look on its face. Myra walked in.

In the corner a bard played lively fiddle music, Myra couldn't be sure, but the bard looked female, something unusual and potentially dangerous in these parts. The place was well lit, and men chattered loudly at most of the tables, bumping mugs into each other in constant toasts to their good health. The barmaid at the counter grinned at Myra, looking her up and down in appraisal. Myra stepped up to the counter, unsure of how she should act with this woman.

"Been travelin' a long time, miss?" Myra considered a response to the question.

She felt a great swirling of emotions. *How long I have been traveling.* she sighed wearily

"Yes-Yes I have." The woman examined her cloak and buckskin breeches

"Where did you buy those *fine* travellin' clothes? I constantly have people coming here asking me what traders to get supplies from, but I've never been out of the city, myself."

Myra could not imagine a life without travel. But that would have been her fate if she had remained a princess. She would have moved to the capital of her husband's lands and probably never leave it again.

"I made the cloak and breeches myself; the rest were gifts to me in my travels."

The woman plunked a mug of beer in front of her.

"It's pretty slow right now,"
Myra glanced at the tables, most of them were full.
"So, tell me, where did you travel from? What are you doing in these parts? Give me the details. Life gets so boring here at times." Myra was about to answer but the woman interrupted.
"It's the stories that keep me going! And I bet you have quite the tale to tell!"
The woman looked her up and down again, leaning in with a full bosom, very prominently displayed by her clothes. Myra averted her eyes.
"I don't wish to go into my story..."
Myra stopped, realizing that's exactly what she would have to do. This woman would be the perfect one to spread the rumors for her.
"But I will tell you some of it." She added, and the woman was hooked. A man stepped up to the bar asking for another beer. She waved him away distractedly not even looking at the man
"You'll have to get Hannah to serve you John. I'm having a most invigorating conversation here."
The man looked at Myra sidelong and harrumphed, then he moved down the bar, yelling to the other barmaid for a beer.

The woman watched her expectantly, Myra shifted, regaining her focus

"Yes, well..." Myra leaned in, not wanting to speak so loudly here, especially after today's ruffled crowd.
"I was one of the sacrificed." The woman's eyebrows shot up.
"I survived by chance really..." her mind drifted back to the day she first saw the wolves. She'd never be able to tell that story, not to these people.
"I began to save children, others who had been sacrificed... But-" Myra's mind butted in; *you tell stories so terribly Myra! Give the details but don't bore them on the unimportant stuff.* Inwardly Myra sighed, already exhausted by the task her mind had given her.
"Girls of all ages and walks of life were sacrificed, left to die

of starvation or from the elements. Some were just toddlers!" Myra leaned back, grief stopping her for a moment.
She took a deep breath,
"I couldn't save them all. There were hundreds that died and most of the girls I saved probably did not make it out of those woods."
The woman exclaimed loudly,
"You SURVIVED the *forbidden* woods?!"
Myra shushed her.
"Yes, now calm down. They aren't so different from any other forest, despite the stories."
Then, a thought struck her, most of *those stories* she had created as a young woman, in an attempt to stop the hunting of her wolves.
She took a moment to let that sink in. Her mind whispered in a surprised way, *maybe you aren't that bad of a storyteller after all...*
"So why did you come *here*? You must have been sacrificed at a fairly young age, or from what I hear rumors of among the people." The woman chattered.
Myra felt her heart crack a little. It was as though the people thought nothing of killing their children. It was just a way of life to them, something you could discuss without breaking into tears.
How strange, Myra thought, *that we should be so disconnected from each other.*
"I came to stop the sacrifices forever... I need you to help me teach the people what really happens to the children, that we don't have to abandon them anymore! The Gods don't want them."
The woman stared at her blankly
"What really happens to the children?"
Myra suppressed a groan; it was hard enough telling this story but to have to explain it in detail would be an ordeal in itself.
Deciding to explain it as simply as possible she said hotly,
"The children die long, slow, painful deaths and are left to rot in the forest, while the Gods do not even care. The Gods, if there

are any, do not accept the offerings!
The children who I managed to save, had to live with the trauma that not only did their parents and their people not want them, the Gods did not either and would not end their suffering!"
Myra realized too late that she was shouting. The tavern was very quiet, and everyone was staring at her. "Sorry, I will go now.", Myra murmured getting off the bar stool. She slunk to the doorway, trying to avert the eyes from her by acting invisible. The bard called to her,
"Wait! Miss, wait! I wish to hear the story you told Marylin."
The bard's voice was thick with an accent, but it carried high over the people gathered in the tavern and Myra knew she could not ignore it. She straightened and stared directly into the bard's eyes across the room. Yep, the bard was definitely a woman. Her face was feminine, but solid, easily passable as a man to an unsuspecting crowd. Myra could see a long wisp of dark brown hair that escaped from her hat and lay upon her shoulder. The bard's eyes were unreadable to Myra, but she seemed welcoming. Myra sat beside her.
The bard leaned forward; Myra could see a single gold hoop in one ear.
"Tell me your story quietly, if you can. I will continue to play, and no one will be able to overhear"
Myra nodded her consent. The bard picked up her fiddle and began to play a slow, melodic tune. Myra began her story. She was nervous of the woman's motives, but she felt the need to tell it to her.
The bard gracefully switched from song to song with little pause between until Myra's story was done. The bard inclined her head to Myra and said loudly "I shall have a short break now and will be back in half an hour." There was a grumble of dismay from some of the patrons but it was a cheerful one. The woman leapt up from her post, putting the fiddle carefully away into a case. Heading up to the bar with the heavy case in hand, the bard said to Marilyn,
"Keep this in the back, if anyone so much as touches it, they'll be

dead! Now give me a beer and I'll pay for her's as well."

Marilyn looked at them suspiciously but inclined her head.

"Here you go" she said a moment later, two fresh mugs of beer in hand.

The bard tossed Marilyn some coins and nodded to the doorway. They sat outside by the steps. It was cool, dusk was growing in the shadows, making the buildings standout in sharp contrast to the sunset sky.

"My name's Willow" the woman said, taking Myra's to kiss it politely as is custom for men. Myra bowed her head, slightly mockingly, but did not give her name. "And *yours* is?" Willow asked, a smirk on her lips.

Myra looked away to the quieting city around them.

"You can call me Marian."

Willow raised an eyebrow but didn't press. She took a long draught of her beer, sighing in contentment. Myra shifted; her old body uncomfortable on the hard-stone steps.

"Why did you bring me out here?" Myra asked.

Willow laughed, setting her beer down.

"Your story was very compelling, and I thank you for telling it to me with such conviction… But, I wonder… How can I trust that what you tell is true?"

Myra felt a faint flare of anger, but, she settled it. It wasn't an attack but rather an honest question.

Myra thought for a while.

"I could show you the graves of the sacrificed… But you would have to enter the forbidden wood."

Willow considered this for a time.

"But, how could you convince them?" the bard gestured back at the tavern,

"or them" she pointed to the tall towers that protected the palace behind.

Myra shrugged, hopelessness rising in her.

"I don't know."

"hmm… Rumors are good ways.." Willow bit her lip thoughtfully,

"Or you could go straight to the Queen and tell her this, but risk being killed for it."

"I already have."

Willow stared at her surprised.

"well... I guess that didn't work then?"

Myra shook her head.

"She disagreed that it should be stopped. She said even if she did change the law that the people would get into an uproar over it and start a rebellion."

Willow sighed.

"Figures"

Myra snorted.

"Yeah... Liana was always a careful girl, probably kept her out of a lot of trouble when she took the throne."

"You knew her before she was Queen?" Willow asked, suspicious.

Myra shook her head. This beer was making her tell truths she did not want to tell.

"Never mind. I was just musing. Now how would you get this story to the people and make it convincing and yet loud enough that the Queen would have to do something?"

Willow blew out her cheeks.

"Well... Lets see, you've told the Queen directly; you've told a barmaid with a loose tongue, a clever bard, and potentially a myriad of others. I think you're on the right track, but it will take some time."

Myra got up, tired of waiting, tired of losing her courage, tired of trying to convince others.

"I've waited thirty years for this to change! Thirty years... I'm tired of waiting for something to happen! I want the law changed *now*, so I can live in *peace*."

Willow looked down at the ground, her voice low.

"I don't think you'll ever have peace, Marian... Not with what you've been through."

Myra swiped tears from her eyes, trying to stay brave "I'm just so tired of seeing nothing happen. I can't bear to see another girl sacrificed to a God that doesn't even exist! I can't *do* this anymore!"

Myra strode off; needing to clear her head, feel fresh air, something. She had to get away from this feeling inside her.

Willow called after her,

"Hey! If you don't have money to pay for a bed tonight, you can ask Marilyn to give you a bed in exchange for work."

Myra called back over her shoulder, barely managing to keep her voice from wobbling from emotion,

"Thanks, I'll be fine."

She could hear the mumbled reply of Willow as she got up and went back to the tavern

"Fine, suit yourself."

Demands

"Your majesty! There's a riot going on in front of the chapel and the priests are quite upset. They want to know what they should do" the page braced a hand on the doorframe of the Queen's study, trying to keep his breath from coming in gasps.

"a *riot*?! How big is this riot?" the Queen turned from a pile of papers she had been inspecting, to look at the messenger.

He was a young lad, probably just reached manhood, by Liana's guess. He fidgeted uncomfortably at her stare. "probably a hundred strong, your majesty"

Liana's eyebrows rose.

"hmm... What are they rioting about? They have tolerable taxes, almost everyone is housed, and we haven't had a spoilage in our food stores for years"

The lad could not look at her, his gaze kept wandering as he spoke. It was as though he was afraid of what she might do when he told her the rest of the story.

"It seems that they're concerned about the laws regarding the worship of the gods... Particularly the god of fertility and-"

"the god of fertility? As in Weirion?"

"yes, your majesty"

"What laws are they particularly concerned with?"

A voice came from behind her.

"I think you already know which one"

Tico stood casually behind the messenger; his arms folded over his chest in an "I told you so" way.

"Do you think Myra started it? Have your men found her yet?"

"I'm certain that Myra is behind this, but there is no evidence that she started it. The person who started it was a young bard who plays in one of the local taverns. One of my men overheard him spreading stories that Weirion wasn't accepting the sacrifices and they had proof of it. I'd not heard word of a riot though. That must have been a spontaneous decision."

Liana turned back to the messenger.

"Thank you for your message. Tell the priests that I will send soldiers down there right away to break it up and restore peace to their chapel. Now be quick"

The lad ran out, sprinting so fast he almost didn't make the corner and narrowly missed running headlong into prince Tico. He apologized over his shoulder and continued.

Liana turned on Tico

"Is there any news? Did they find her in the forest?"

"No, her cabin was empty and looked shut up for a while, the wolves were nowhere to be found."

Liana growled in frustration

"It's been too long since I knew her well… I have no idea what she plans to do next"

"We'll find her", Tico promised.

Later, Liana decided it would be good to show her presence to the people by going to the chapel herself to check on the priests now that the riot had been broken up. It had been a while since she had given offerings to the god Weirion and it would do well for her to show her continued loyalty to the god.

She rode on a steel grey mare. Liana's blue gown was embroidered with spiraling vines and flowers. It draped elegantly on her mare. She sat straight in the saddle, looking proud and dangerous to mess with. But, inside, a thought clawed at her. It crawled up her spine and itched at her mind. She tried to flick it away, but it continued to crawl through her mind until it surfaced, making her heart pang.

It was the memory of her rides with Myra, when they had galloped through the fields outside the city. Their guards would cringe and yell at them to slow down. An unbidden grin spread across Liana's lips. Her sister was still alive. But the thought twisted to an ugly snarl. *Now you'll have to execute her for starting a potentially lethal rebellion. She just wanted the sacrifices to stop. You can't let them stop.*

The memory of her father returning with the hunting party, Russet's reins in his hands, her saddle empty of her rider, crushed her every time. Fighting back the memories she returned to the present. The people stood to each side of her, their faces grim. No one smiled, no one waved. They just stood like statues of judgement.

I'm too old for this. Liana thought tiredly.

Finally, they made it to the chapel. The priests greeted her with relieved bows and smiles. Liana could see the hulking statue of Weirion sitting like a thundercloud behind the white chapel walls. Liana dismounted, handing her horse off to a stable boy. She greeted the priests and they accompanied her into the chapel. It was a grand building with high vaulted ceilings depicting beautiful paintings of the gods and their heroic deeds.

The main entrance to the chapel was dedicated to the god Weirion, with other rooms dedicated to the lesser gods and goddesses.

Weirion was atop a magnificent horse carved mid-leap as its hooves were just about to crash down upon a wolf. The wolf's teeth were exaggerated, and it was caught in a howl of pain as it was stabbed by Weirion's lance. The wolf was deathly looking, its bones jutting out under its pelt.

This was a more unusual rendition of the hunt that Weirion took, to bring fertility to the earth. The wolf's blood was said to bring power to the one who drank it. However, if you looked into the wolf's eyes then you would be cursed forever.

On the statue, the wolf's eyes were shut, so that no one would really know what the wolf's eyes might have looked like to cause such a terrible curse.

Liana stood before it, her guards surrounding her without getting in the way of her view of the statue. She knelt, kissing the floor at the statue's feet. She whispered quietly, so that her guards may not overhear. "Lord Weirion show me guidance in this answer that I seek. I know that my sister would not want to cause harm, but I cannot let her tear down the kingdom" She stared into the god's eyes, it stared blankly into the space between. Narrowly stopping herself from cursing at the statue she whispered harshly "Show me what to do! My judgement is clouded, and I need your guidance!" The statue did not miraculously change into a man, nor did a loud voice boom over the city to give her guidance.

It remained a statue.

She stood, lowered her head in reverence and stormed out of the hall.

Her guards caught up to her clipped pace, their clanging armor loudly ringing in the acoustics of the building.

When Liana returned to the palace there was a stir of excitement. She could feel it hanging in the room. Turning to the captain of her guard she said,

"What news of my sister? Have you found any trace of her?"

The guard inclined his head.

"Your Majesty, we have no news of your sister but the bard who started the riot this morning has been caught and is currently being held in the cells."

Liana nodded, starting towards the throne room.

"Bring him to me, I wish to question him of his motives."

"As you wish your Majesty." the captain bowed and passed on her order to another guard.

Liana walked into the throne room. Servants disappeared out of the corner of her vision as she entered. It was always quite the skill to make yourself invisible to the Queen. She was constantly surprised at their adeptness.

She sighed and sat upon the throne, her body aching terribly from her short excursion. Moments later a commotion outside the hall gained her attention. Her guards inside the hall gathered around her whilst a few others opened the large doors to find what was the matter. Just outside the doors squirmed a young lad. The lad had a traditional, long braid that reminded

Liana of the Vikings to the north. One of the guards who'd opened the door yelled at the others fumbling with boy.

"Control him! You put our Queen in danger!"

The guards quickly got the lad under control. Even from Liana's perch, far across the hall, she could hear the constant muttering of curse words from the wayward boy. A guard cuffed him, and he stopped.

"Your Majesty, this is the bard who we believe started the riot this morning."

"What do you play?" Liana asked the lad. Everyone seemed confused by the question. The bard replied, "The lute miss-I-I mean your Majesty. I play the lute and sing." She nodded.

"Did you confiscate his instrument as well?"

The guards exchanged glances.

"We only found a fiddle your Majesty. No lute to be seen."

"Hmmm... Why would you lie boy?"

The lad seemed to be racing for an answer.

"I-I traded my lute for a fiddle your majesty. The fiddle was in fine condition and I had only my lute for payment. The man took it otherwise he was just going to burn the poor instrument, he thought it had a curse on it".

"Bring the fiddle. We'll see if the man tells the truth. You told me that the man we're looking for plays the fiddle regularly in the local inns?"

A guard stepped forward, "Yes your majesty. This was the bard we found at the tavern."

"Who sold you the fiddle boy?"

The lad looked up at her, eyes bright with life.

"Willow... Willow was his name. He didn't give any other name I'm afraid... Your majesty."

The Queen looked over to the guard.

"Does this match with your bard?"

The guard looked uncomfortable.

"Yes your majesty, the bard's name was Willow and he played fiddle."

"Why then did you bring me this boy?!", she asked impatiently

"He matched the same description as the bard we were searching for. He also had the fiddle in his possession."
The Queen turned sharply to the boy.
"Play the fiddle. We'll see if you are him or, not."
The lad looked between the guards and the Queen. A guard brought the bard the fiddle. The bard handled it awkwardly, fumbling with the bow. Finally getting himself somewhat organized he raised the bow with a trembling hand and, with a look of extreme concentration played a scratchy, squealing note. The Queen winced but nodded for the bard to continue. It was painful and unmelodious to say the least and the Queen bid him to stop.
"I see now that you have no training in the art of playing the fiddle. You are released from custody, but we will be keeping an eye on you."
She warned before the guards took him away.

Willow narrowly bolted out of the palace gates when the guards let her go, but she managed to keep herself to a calm walk until she got out of sight of the guards. Her fiddle clutched tightly in her arms, she trotted through the throngs of people in the market, dodging market stands and scampering around small children.
Finally, she made it to the back of a large old warehouse that used to repair wagons, now shut down and abandoned. She knocked twice on the door and it swung open just enough for

her to slip in.

Hannah closed the door behind her. The barmaid was a tall, big-boned woman; someone you would not want to mess with. She leaned against the door, sighing in relief.

"I thought you'd never make it out of that place alive!"

"Well, I'm still alive and well!" Willow said cheerfully laughing, despite her shaking hands and hammering heart.

Hannah did not laugh.

Instead she walked past Willow to a table and chairs that were set up in a corner of the warehouse. The warehouse is largely populated with various wagon parts and the floor is littered with dust, hay, old mouse droppings and broken wheels.

Willow follows Hannah and gestures to the meat and bread laid out on the table.

"Can I have some?"

"No. Not until you tell me how you managed to get caught, released and still have your hide and your fiddle!"

Willow smiled slyly. "I fooled them with very, very poor fiddle-playing skills."

"And they *believed* you!?"

Willow laughed.

"Crazily enough yes! It was really just a lucky coincidence!"

Hannah crossed her arms, her face growing stern. "Why did you make yourself so obvious? They could have killed you and we would have risked our necks for naught."

"I'm sorry I just-"

"I wasn't finished! You won't be able to go out where you can be seen. At least not looking like you do. You're too distinctive."

Willow shrugged her shoulders.

"What do you suggest I do?"

"Cut that mane of yours and look like a lady for once!"

Willow gawked at her. "Cut my hair? But I spent the last *ten years* growing it out! And for your information, it wasn't *my* idea to dress as a man and go around as a common bard."

"That idea has to change now. You need to look like a common peasant woman, someone who will blend in with the crowd and

not be suspicious."
Willow sighed,
"Where's the dress I must wear. I am your humble servant."
Hannah laughed. "It's in the loft. When you're ready I've some shears to tame your forelock."
Willow laughed, climbing the ladder to the loft, she added "I may never be ready for the day you take the shears to my hair. I cringe at what they'll do."
"Don't worry. We'll make a proper lady of you yet!"

Liana had constant memories of Myra running through her head these days. At each turn in the palace she could remember her little sister splashing in the fountain, or their games of hide and seek. Then, when they were older, Liana had taught her the behavior of dogs and how to handle them. They would spend long hours in the kennels caring for the dogs.
After Myra had been sacrificed, Liana could not bear to see the dogs and had gotten rid of many of them, except those used by her sisters for hunting. As for Liana, she never went hunting again.
Now Myra was gone again. Probably fled to the forest. Liana could still hear her last words to Myra echoing in her head.
"I should have had you executed when you returned. Yet, I spared you, though it goes against my better judgement."
Then, Myra's expression. She was crushed. The flash of betrayal that had flashed across her face as she had replied curtly,
"I will not be back again" and that was the last Liana had seen of

her.

Where are you, Myra? Where would you have gone? Liana can feel the hollowness of grief opening below her like a pit, threatening to swallow her.

Liana tried to return to the task at hand; she was in council about the riots breaking out across the city. Suddenly, the people were demanding that the law be changed to stop the sacrifices. She still had no guidance from Weirion. It was empty inside her mind. Only the memories of her sister flitted around in the back of her mind.

Tico cut short her reverie in the memories.

"My Lady, Liana? What is your opinion in this matter?"

Liana stirred, regretting her absent mind, for she had no idea what conversation was happening. She blurted, before her mind caught up to her,

"I think we should stop the killings. It's only right that we should listen to the people. They are the ones having to deal with the grief of their loved ones. I have asked council from our Lord Weirion, but all I hear is silence. My heart tells me we should stop this."

The table of councilors and royal subjects stared at her, gawking slightly.

Micareon, her Lord Councilor, cleared his throat,

"Is it wise, your majesty? Should we seek council of the priests? It might be that Lord Weirion is simply biding his time until the right moment comes?"

Liana shook her head.

"I apologize for not thinking my statement further before speaking but I still stand by my belief. Lord Weirion can't be trusted to speak at all. He hasn't spoken for at least a hundred years if the priests' records are anything to go by. No. We must take action now or risk the kingdom being torn apart by internal wars."

Tico stood, his eyes growing dark with anger.

"Mother! You cannot change a law just because it fits your fancy! You are not the only one to have lost a loved one to the sacrifices. But if we stop, there will be the rage of the Gods upon us and that would be far worse than a war inside our country's borders!"

"The Zorlanders grow stronger every day and threaten to overtake our country to east and the Southlanders are angry that we have ceased trade along their borders. If we take action or not, we will have chaos anyway! Better to be struck down by the Gods than be cowardly and risk losing everything because we didn't change!"

Liana stood. Complete silence covered the hall. She almost checked her ears to make sure she hadn't had a lapse of hearing. Then, a sharp inhale of breath from Micareon. It felt like a bellow in the silence.

"Your Majesty, I implore you to think this through further. What you do will affect thousands of people! It could be the destruction of the kingdom!"

"Lord Micareon, I thank you for your concern, but I have made my decision. We have had this law since before my father's time. Millions of girls have been sacrificed to the Gods as recompense. Has it really done us any good?"

"Your majesty!" someone exclaimed.

"We still are on the edge of war, both inside and outside our borders. Our riches and economy are dwindling. It is only a matter of time before something has to change. Why not break this tradition and change the law? Maybe Weirion will be pleased by our actions and give us great fortunes!"

Tico stared at her. "Have you gone utterly mad? What you do will destroy us! I cannot stand for this!" and he went out of the hall in a huff.

Liana looked at her council, their faces were grim and disapproving. "I stand by my word." she said defensively.

Fredrick, the eldest of the council, murmured "Let us just hope its not your last" as he strode out. The others followed, sending suspicious glances back at her.

"The meeting is adjourned." she nearly spat.
"Ludicrous old dogs!" she grumbled, storming to her chambers.

Liana strode quickly towards her chambers, calling out to one of her messengers. "Birkitt! Send a letter to my councilors that I will make preparations to change this law by the end of the week. Also get word sent to the people that any children this week who have been chosen to be sacrificed will be pardoned. Lord Weirion forgive me should I be rash in this decision."

Reconciliation

The crowds were thick around the palace. The acrid smell of human sweat mixed with the stench of unwashed bodies. It was loud on ground level. People were all trying to talk over each other as they discussed what was going to happen. A nervous energy held taut in the air and Willow could feel the hairs on her neck stand on end. Or maybe it was because there was no hair there to block the wind. Hannah had sheared Willow's hair into a shoulder-length cut and today had pinned Willow's thick, black hair into a bonnet. Willow still hated how short it was now. She felt so exposed.

Staring up at the balcony where the royals would make their grand announcements, Willow could feel a certain ominous air about the place. She looked up to the walls and towers surrounding the balcony. It was crammed with guards and soldiers, arrows aimed towards the crowd. Willow let out a low whistle.
"They must be worried about an uproar.", she mused to the large hulk that was Hannah.
"Mmm..." was her reply.
"Marian coming?" Hannah asked casually.
"Dunno... I saw her back in the city just a few days ago. Pretty nervy. I hope she doesn't show up, we already have enough problems going on right now without Marian causing a scene."
Hannah nodded, then walked off into the crowd.
"Hey! Where are *you going*?" Willow tried to run after her, but Hannah continued on as if she hadn't heard.

Suddenly, trumpets blared the announcement of the Queen and everyone clapped and cheered as they were supposed to. Willow felt torn. She should stay here so that no one would say that she was guilty for any of the Queen's decision. So, she watched as Hannah disappeared into the crowd.

Looking up at the Queen she could see the wear that this role had on the Queen now. She looked so tired, so weak and vulnerable before them. Queen Liana raised her hands almost in defeat of the applause and everyone was silent. You could hear a horse whinnying far in the distance.

Pince Tico did not stand beside her on the balcony. It was only she and her guards. When she did speak it rung out over the crowd and startled Willow. She hadn't been prepared for the loud, strong voice that came from this frail Queen.

"People of Belloc, my people of Gandalon. Today is a day to rejoice! The Gods have spoken and given wisdom to me that I will give to you dear people."

Willow sighed, *why won't she just get on with it!*

"The sacrifices from this day forth will stop. The Gods do not wish for our young maidens to pacify them. They wish for us to work together with our fellow countries and bring abundance and prosperity to all"

"Rubbish!",

"You've gone mad my Queen!",

"The Gods will make you pay for this!", people shouted. Willow was shocked at their directness. *The Queen's power must truly be slipping for them to be so bold!*

The Queen put up her hands, growing fierce.

"Peace! The Gods have spoken, and I am their messenger. Rejoice that your daughters will not have to die in vain!"

Someone in the crowd shouted to her, their voice weary "Then what say you of the ones already sacrificed? Are their deaths worthless? How could you ever make up for that loss!"

The Queen looked down for a moment, seeming to gather herself.

When she spoke, her voice wavered slightly with emotion.

"I cannot bring back the lives of those we lost, though, if there were a way I could undue this madness I would. I too lost a loved one to the sacrifices. Some of you may remember my youngest sister... Princess Myrianna" Her voice grew quiet, yet it still carried.

"Known to most as Myra"

The crowd was suddenly silent.

Then an oddly familiar woosh sliced through the air. Willow looked around trying to understand the sound. Then a cry burst out from the balcony and the thump of an arrow.

Willow looked quickly to the Queen and a cry escaped her lips. An arrow protruded from the Queen's chest, she stood still for a moment. Her face was screwed with surprise and pain. A guard quickly caught her as she fell. Screams and yells filled the echoing courtyard. Willow stared a moment longer at the Queen, before Liana was surrounded by her guards. People ran like ants scampering over each other to try and get out. Guards barred the way and forced them back.

"You aren't allowed to leave until we find who did this!" The guards pointed spears at them and others had many bows trained on them from above. Suddenly Hannah was beside her.

"We need to get out of here! Now!"

Before Willow could try and get an answer out of her of where she'd been Hannah had dragged her into a back entrance. The guards had not gotten organized yet for that entrance, so they slipped through unnoticed.

Hannah wove them through back alley after back alley until they got to the warehouse.

Shoving her inside Hannah slammed the door behind them.

"Did anyone follow us?" she asked, breathless.

"I don't think so." Willow realized she was shaking, and she was caught by lightheadedness. She sat down on the hay covered floor.

"Did you...Did *you* do this?!" She accused Hannah

Hannah tried to pacify her,

"Shhh it's not the time to discuss what might have happened. Here, take my shawl. You're freezing! I'll get you something to drink."

"Hannah! Did you or did you not just *assassinate* the Queen?"

Hannah would not look at her. She kept her back to Willow as she tried to find a flask.

"The less you know, the better."

"Oh my GODS HANNAH! You *killed the Queen*?!"

Hannah whipped around.

"Shut up! You're going to get us killed if you keep your voice up like that!"

Willow could feel the earth moving under her feet like water. She set out a hand to steady herself. Her whole world had just been turned upside down.

"Oh my Gods… What have you done?" she breathed; her mind swirling like a whirlwind.

"I did what had to be done!" Hannah said defensively.

Myra rushed towards the castle, tears skittering off her cheeks.

"Liana. Liana!" she whimpered, pushing past dawdling people in the lane up to the palace.

The guards stopped her at the gates. "Sorry miss, no one is allowed in right now."

"Please! She's my sister!" Myra tried to push past them, her mind lost in emotion.

"I'm Myrianna Martenlander, fifth daughter of the King of Belloc. Please! Let me see her. I have to see her."

"Miss, please!" the guard said, looking around.

"You can't come in."

He looked to the other guard.

"Jordan, get the corporal. I need to seek his council on this one." The other nodded and trotted off.

The guard pushed Myra away and held his spear towards her.

"Please miss, back away. You'll have to wait until the corporal gets here. I have strict orders to not let anyone in."

"PLEASE!! My sister is dying! I can't let her die alone!" Myra's knees buckled and she sobbed uncontrollably. "Oh, Liana! Oh my Gods, Liana." she whimpered.

The guard shifted uncomfortably in front of her, avoiding eye contact and pretending as if she wasn't there.

Finally, another man came up, he had a greying beard that was closely cropped. He wore a black uniform with the gold insignia of the Gandalon kingdom. His face was severe; it was hard to tell whether the man had any joy within him at all.

"What's going on here Miles? This woman is in hysterics!"

"Corporal Isenford, thank the Gods you're here! This woman is demanding to see the Queen. She claims that she's her sister."

The man walked up to Myra, who had her face shrouded by dreaded hair.

"Stand, woman. What proof have you that you are related in any way to the Queen of Gandalon?"

Myra looked up at him through her hair and her hands. Her face was hollow, tears streaked her cheeks but her eyes were what sent a shiver down Miles' back. They showed the tortured soul beneath; haunted by years of loneliness, hurt, and abandonment. He stepped back but could not break eye contact with her.

"Please, let me see my sister, before I never have the chance to do so again."

Corporal Isenford was going to press the matter further but a voice hollowed by grief spoke behind him.

"Let her come. She doesn't have much time." It was George, the Queen's most trusted of her personal guard.

"Come with me, Lady Myra"

He stepped over to Myra's crumpled form and held out a hand to help her up.

"George! You cannot undermine my authority like this! You will be excused from the army if you follow through with this!" Corporal Isenford nearly spat at George in fury.

George looked up at the corporal, his eyes like a sad dog who'd just lost their master.

"I don't care anymore corporal. My Queen is dying and I have no wish to continue on, for I've failed her. I failed her when she needed it most. So, there's nothing here I want any more... I

should have taken that arrow. If only I had realized sooner."
The corporal tried to fight the point but was wordless. He watched, angrily as George led Myra gently past him and into the palace beyond.
Myra was silent. Her head lowered.
"Thank you." She said quietly.
"*Of course...* Liana... Queen Liana is not well. She's very weak from blood loss and the arrow..." He let out a long shaky breath "The arrow punctured her lung, so she hasn't long."
Myra tried to keep herself together but when she looked up at the guard and saw his eyes were shiny with tears she could not hold the sobs in any longer.
He led her quietly through the palace and to the hallway of the Queen's chambers. Guards stood at the entrance, their eyes shining, but no tears fell. They had all loved the Queen. She had always been kind and fair to them. She was the shining, brilliant sun that they had all taken for granted.
Healers went in and out of the room, bringing fresh towels and returning ones soiled with blood to the kitchens.
Myra had recovered a bit by then. She stopped and let go of the guard's arm. Turning to him she said shakily "The devotion and love you have for my sister, is unmistakable. You have gone above and beyond your duties as a guard and I know you hold yourself responsible. Forgive yourself... for her... and for me. There was nothing you could have done, and I know that my sister's time has been numbered for quite a while. You have brought her hope in our future and I thank you from the bottom of my heart." George wiped away tears, unabashed by his grief.
Chokingly, he replied, "Thank you" and backed away from the doors. The other guards looked at her warily, but George nodded that it was ok.
They gingerly opened the doors.
What struck Myra first was the smell; blood and the sickly-sweet smell of herbs stung her nose like a punch to the face. She could identify plantain, comfrey and yarrow among the smells. Next what struck her was the sight. There was a large bed that

occupied most of the chamber.

The top sheets were soaked red with blood. Below them lay a small bump, then she could see Liana's head propped up on pillows. Her white hair and already pale complexion made her face bone white. Myra had to suppress a sobbing gulp. She straightened her back, rolled her shoulders back and with tears streaming rivers down her cheeks she walked quietly to the bed. Healers surrounded her, some barking orders to others to bring more bandages. By the window stood Tico, his face hidden from Myra. She could see from his posture that he wasn't in a good space right then. Trying to push back a wave of lightheadedness and nausea, Myra stood by the bed. A healer looked up at her, his eyes pitiful.

"How much longer does she have?" Myra asked, her voice sounded dead to her ears.

"An hour maybe more if we can stop the bleeding. But, the arrow pierced her lung and she is bleeding inside." Myra nodded, unable to speak.

Liana's eyes were shut, and her breath came in nightmarish rasps; gurgling slightly from the blood in her lungs. Myra had to hold herself steady lest she run out of the room screaming and never get a chance to speak to her sister ever again.

"Liana… Liana I just want you to know that I love you. I wish for nothing more in the world that to have us galloping across the countryside with the hunting dogs, in pursuit of the hunt. I wish we could be so, so far away from here" Myra choked on her tears. Liana's eyes opened. They seemed to fight through a crusty layer of salt from tears, as they began to focus. Her stunning grey-blue eyes looked up at Myra.

"Myra!?" Liana croaked incredulously. Myra knelt leaning closer to her sister

"I'm here! Oh Gods, Liana, I'm here!" Liana's eyes grew shiny with tears

"I'm sorry for what I said. I never wanted anything more than to see you come out of those woods and be by my side. I let you down"

Myra shook her head, tears flying off her cheeks

"No Liana, *I'm* sorry. I should have come sooner! We could have had so much more time." Myra couldn't stop the sobs. She felt Liana's hand reach for hers, she grasped it. Liana's grip was weak, and her hand was cold, but it felt so comforting to hold it in her hands.

Liana struggled to adjust her head, gasping in pain "Shh... stay still!", Myra said trying to keep her from hurting herself further. Liana turned her head slightly and glared in annoyance, before breaking into a weak grin.

Myra laughed wetly, "You've always been a stubborn one, sister."

Liana's face grew serious. "Myra, there's something you must promise me."

Liana glanced at the window where Tico had been. He was gone. She turned back to Myra, her voice came in rasps, and she coughed several times, sending blood into her mouth.

"Myra, I hate to ask this of you..." rattling cough, "You must never let Tico reach the throne. He will destroy himself and the kingdom. You must exile him to the forbidden forest. There, he will find himself." She stopped for a moment, gathering strength. "When the people find out that he was behind my death they will hunt him down. He will be safer in the forest"

Myra clutched Liana's hand harder. *Tico!? Behind Liana's murder?* "Are you sure Tico was behind this?" Myra asked, incredulous.

Liana stared at Myra, seemingly as her only answer. Then, gathering a rattling breath that caught in a cough, she whispered, "I saw him loose the arrow..." she seemed to want to say more but she lost her strength. They sat quietly for a time; Liana's breath came in the bone-chilling rattle of death. A healer woman touched Myra's shoulder gently.

"She doesn't have much time. I suggest you make your goodbyes" Myra nodded, trying to swallow past the emotions that engulfed her.

Liana's eyes fluttered open for a moment "Do not let him be hung. His soul is lost, and I need you to bring it back to him...

Send him to the forests, where he will not do damage to others. He will come back to himself in time."

Myra swept tears from her eyes. "Did you know he was going to kill you?"

Liana blinked, swallowing slowly, as if it was difficult for her to keep from coughing. "Yes... I knew it from the time you entered the kingdom."

"AND YOU DIDN'T STOP IT!? You could have saved your life!" Myra yelled, anger, fear and grief whirling within her.

"My dear Myra... A queen's life doesn't belong to her. Her country's safety is always paramount to her own. If I had brought it to the attention of my council Tico could have spun the story to sound as if I've gone mad and he could have taken the throne. This way I can die in peace knowing he will never reach the throne."

"But what about me? I never wished to rule Gandalon! I only wished for the sacrifices to stop!"

"Precisely why you will make the best leader, my dear sister."

"How dare you assume I will take this position! I don't want it. I have no wish to meddle in the affairs of the country! I just want to be with my wolves in peace!"

Liana shut her eyes; she was almost too weak to speak.

"Leave me, Myra. See your wolves. Live your life. We've said this last goodbye too many times. I don't wish you to see me take my last breath."

She coughed terribly and Myra stepped back. It took her a long moment before she could let go of Liana's hand. Her anger disappeared in an instant as she saw her sister lying weakly on the bed, blood dribbling from the corner of her mouth. She leaned in close to Liana, speaking with all the love and memories she could muster of her sister. "Go now in peace dear sister. Join our sisters in the afterlife, enjoy the time that was forsaken you... Take care of Layrn till my time comes... I love you"

Then Myra ran out. She'd witnessed many deaths but this one was too hard to be a part of any longer.

She rushed past the guards, down the corridors and finally made

it to the courtyard where she sat panting under a large willow. She sat there in complete stillness for a long time; her eyes staring off into space, her face expressionless, until she heard the death toll of the bells. They rang loud over the kingdom and Myra crumpled into body-wracking sobs.
There was nothing she could do now.

Corroboration

Willow wandered the streets. She felt like the whole world had been tipped upside down and shaken.

When she'd heard the death tolls, she'd known that this wasn't all just a bad dream. No… This was worse than any nightmare she'd ever had or could have imagined.

Now the bloodthirsty son of their beloved Queen would take the throne. Prince Tico had always made Willow's hackles raise. There was something not right in that man.

She bypassed the market. She wasn't in the mood for that many people; that many, just moving on with life, while the kingdom had just lost their Queen.

Willow could feel a wave of anger hit her. *How dare they!* Just before her mind went off in a rant, she spotted Myra.

"Marian!" she called, her mood quickly changing from anger to joy at seeing a familiar face.

Myra was dressed in a simple black gown, her hair hung sickly upon her head, reflecting the mood of the woman.

She raised her head, like a bone-weary dog, hearing its master call its name.

"Oh, it's you" Myra said, a ghost of a smile appearing on her aged face.

Willow hurried over to her. "Are you ill, Marian? You look like death warmed over!"

Myra shook her head "No… I… I-I've been in mourning of our Queen. Her death has taken a terrible…" She took a deep breath seeming to control herself, "terrible toll on me."

Willow felt her heart go out to this woman. She looked so old and almost delirious with grief.

"Come, let me take you to the tavern. I'll get you a drink."

Myra tried to pull away from her, "No Willow, thank you for the offer, I should be heading back to the palace now."
Willow stopped, "The palace?! Are-are you an informant?"
Myra could see Willow recoil in fear and judgement and felt a twang in her heart. She laughed helplessly, "No, Willow. I'm no informant... But I can't-", she paused. "I can't tell you at this time who I am, but please trust me."
Willow stared are her bewildered.
"I must go now. I'll see you around, old friend." Myra patted Willow's shoulder as she walked past.
Willow watched stunned, as the old woman hobbled down the street and around the corner.

Myra reached the castle, exhausted by her excursions in the city. George trotted up to her. "Thank the Gods! I thought we'd lost you to the woods. The council wishes to adjourn a meeting with Prince Tico and yourself since you are both the closest relatives to... the Queen."
Myra nodded, not caring anymore. She had no energy to argue. "I wish to have a private audience with the council first. I have important information that they need to hear. But first I must rest. I have no energy to ramble on with the courtly niceties that'll be expected of me."
George bowed in reply "I'll ask the captain to assign guards to you. As a relative of the royal court your life could be in danger."
Myra walked away throwing her hands into the air in disgust. She said, "So be it!"

The council sat like vultures around the table. Their mouths watering at where their power might lead them. Myra strode in, her hair was piled onto her head in an elegant braid. She wore a simple black gown. The council started muttering to each other like hens after they've laid an especially large egg. "I'm Myrian Martenlander, fifth daughter of Lord Belloc, the late King of Gandalon." She announced, her voice loud and commanding. She stood watching their muttering grow louder. "If you have something you wish to say about me, to me, or against me, speak louder so I may hear. I have no time for whispered gossip." The council members straightened.

Micareon, Lord Councilor cleared his throat. "I don't wish to offend but, weren't you supposedly killed in sacrifice over thirty years ago?"

Myra smiled tightly, "Yes, and I survived. Now I'm back to right the wrongs in this country. I am a worthy ruler for Gandalon."

The room immediately hushed.

Micareon spoke again "What proof have you that you are truly the blood relative of Queen Liana?"

Myra threw down her fist hard on the table, making the councilors jump in surprise. "All I've been asked since I came into this retched place is who I am; If I am Princess Myra, how I'm not Princess Myra and what should or should not happen to me! Queen Liana, may her soul rest peacefully, believed I am who I claim to be. The mark of the Southlands medicine woman bids that I never lie to the court! If you do not believe me, I don't think I will ever be able to convince you." She sat with that, and watched as the room sat in stunned silence.

Finally, a slightly braver councilor, a younger man, probably in his thirties spoke "I seem to recall that any sacrifices who return are to be executed lest they start a-" he almost choked on the irony and trailed off muttering the last of his sentence "...A rebellion."

"Yes, and Queen Liana spared me, though she admitted that it was against her judgement as Queen."

Eyebrows raised across the table.

The councilor said quietly "I see..."

Micareon spoke again, "Why have you called a private audience with us Lady Myrianna? Is there something you wish to keep from Prince Tico?"

Myra looked to the floor, scratching at the irritating pins that held her hair in place. *Who was she kidding? She would never make a good Queen. But, she didn't have much choice in the matter. Gods this was hard.*

"Queen Liana spoke to me on her deathbed of.." how should she word this?

"Queen Liana believed that she was killed by her son, Lord Tico."

An uproar swept through the room. Finally, Micareon rose, his long robes billowing back. "What proof have you! This is a terribly risky accusation!"

Myra rose too, and quietly spoke. "Queen Liana said she saw him loose the arrow. As we all know Lord Tico has always been an especially talented bowman, even as a boy. She said she had expected that he was going to go after her for some time. She knew for certain when I first entered the court. She believed that he felt threatened by my appearance and when she changed the law of the sacrifices that took him over the tipping point."

The councilors argued amongst themselves, loudly protesting and others agreeing. Finally, they turned to Myra again "Why didn't she bring it before us earlier?"

Myra sat again, feeling as though a great tension had been re-

leased from the air despite the conflict among the councilors. "She was afraid that Tico would spin the tale to look as though her wizening mind had gone around the bend."
The councilors grew loud in their protests, but Myra couldn't focus on their conversations. She was focusing too hard on breathing. It was difficult to speak of Liana's death so soon after she had died.
Two guards positioned themselves beside her. Myra could feel her breath catch and her hackles rise. Micareon addressed her "Until we have further proof that you are actually the Queen's sister in blood, I'm afraid we will have to keep you under arrest. We shall hold you until we have decided that you pose no threat to the royal line. Prince Tico has already warned us of your quick temper and we do not wish to put him or anyone else in danger. I suggest you find someone to be your spokesperson or find greater evidence to prove your case."
The guards then grabbed both of her arms. "Wait! George! The guard, he knows me! He will vouch for me. This is a big mistake! You're arresting the wrong person!"
Micareon's steely gaze bore into hers "We shall see."

Then she was dragged from the room. The guards took her through corridor after corridor and then down a steep stone staircase. The stones were cold, and the chill soaked up through Myra's boots.
I might as well be dead now. Myra thought numbly as they gently pushed her into a cell.
"Sorry, M'lady... I hope this will all be figured out soon. Is there anyone I can contact for you?" The guard's voice was very deep. He was a tall, heavy-built man. He looked oddly familiar, but she couldn't place where she had seen him before. Her mind raced, who could get her out of this mess? Who did she still know? Who knew her past? Then the thought hit her. Julia! But would she even remember Mira, after all, she'd been so little.
"I know of someone, but I know not what the name of the town is that they reside. The town is far to the east of the forbidden

forest. It's small and might have disappeared but could you send a letter to Julia? Addressed from Myra. Tell her I'm in need of her help as I once helped her, so long ago."

"That seems like a pretty big shot in the dark... But I'll try. I think the town's name is Flairen or something the like. I'll let George know that the council put you down here. He'll probably be able to help you more than I."

The guard closed the iron bar door and watched her for a moment.

"Thank you." She whispered, relieved.

He ground his teeth slightly, he came up to the bars, whispering harshly "I will not let that monster take the throne! Not while I still live! You are the rightful heir and I will never fail to stop that man from stealing the throne from you."

The guard leaned back, nodded and left. She could hear his boots thumping up the stone stairs and then silence.

Messages

Farrell ran into the cottage "Julia! Julia, we've gotten a letter! It's addressed to you!"

Julia looked up startled, her hands poised over a ball of dough; just about to punch the bubbling yeast into the bread. "What?" she said, still trying to understand what Farrell had said.

"The-the Queen's sister has sent us a letter! Well I mean she sent you a letter... Here." He handed it to her, almost quivering with excitement. For a grown man, he could get quite riled up sometimes.

She grabbed it with her wrists so as not to get dough on the envelope. She dropped it on the table and washed her hands. "Did Chad give it to you? I thought all the Queen's relatives were dead."

Farrell shrugged "I thought so too, but it is addressed from Princess Myrianna Martenlander. Or, so Chad said." Farrell had never learned how to read.

"I don't believe it! This must be some awful joke." She ripped open the seal and drew out the letter.

To Julia of Fairen.
From Princess Myrianna Martenlander, sister of Liana Martenlander,
the Queen of Gandalon.
Dear Julia, I do hope dearly that your memory will be sparked by

this letter.

This is a long shot. But, here it goes.

I am Myra, the girl who saved you in the forbidden forest when you were just a child. You may remember the wolves more than I... Perhaps you remember my beloved dog Layrn, who used to adore you to bits!

I, too, was sacrificed to Weirion not long before you. I was only sixteen. The last time I saw you was in the town of Fairen. I pray that you are still there and recall me, even in the faintest of memories.

I am in dire need of your help. I hope that I can ask this of you, though I wish I could leave you to continue living in peace. I know it's been such a long time.

I need you to come to the Capital city of Belloc. I am in a dire state. The palace believes that I killed my own sister to take the throne. Though I realize now that the news may not have hit you yet. Regardless, I am innocent. I need your help to convince the council of the court that I truly am Myrianna Martenlander, fifth daughter of Lord Belloc, the late king of Gandalon.

I know that you didn't know me as a Princess but if I have proof that someone knew me whilst I lived in the forbidden woods it may save my life.

I trust that this letter will find you well and that you will be able to help me.

It may mean the survival of Gandalon... Though I understand if you do not come.

May the moon guide you.

-Myra

"What does it say?" Farrell tried to peer over her shoulder despite the fact that he couldn't read.

"It looks important."

Julia could feel tears swelling in her eyes. *Why am I crying?! I don't have any connection to this woman!* She was born in Fairen. She'd married Farrell, her childhood friend from the village. She had never lived with a woman in the forbidden forest!

But, even as her mind tried to fight against this new information, her heart rang with truth. She felt a memory crawling at the back of her mind. She could remember a white dog, who always stared into her eyes as if trying to read her soul. She remembered someone; a kind woman. She'd always thought it was her mother. Bridgit had raised her from a young age but had always told her that she wasn't her mother. She had told her that her mother had been a kind, brave woman who couldn't take care of her anymore.

What if that woman had been this Myra? She had often had dreams as a young child of the forest. Often, they were nightmares of giant man-eating beasts and death reapers on horseback; tearing down her family in front of her. But, sometimes she would have the lingering memory of a gentle dream, of playing in the forest with big, kind dogs.

She sat, stunned. Farrell knelt before her; concern etched into his features. "What's wrong? What is the letter about? You're white as a ghost!"

She shook herself. This was all too much right now. "The Princess has requested my presence in Belloc. She claims that I can help her save the kingdom."

Farrell rocked back on his heels. "Well! That is unexpected to say the least."

She gave a quiet bark of laughter "I'll say!"

Julia stood, dressed in her finest dress. She could feel the eyes of many royals upon her and she felt ashamed at arriving in such a simple gown.

She stepped up to the dais where the Prince sat. He appeared to almost slouch as he considered her. He looked like a very lazy, very dangerous man. Julia swallowed. How she wished Farrell was by her side at this moment. His tall bulk behind her would be comforting. He had stayed behind to mind the farm and the household. It was his insistence that had brought her here before the Prince. She curtsied, bowing low to the Prince. He said in a bored voice "Rise." She stood, brushing off her skirt. She waited, knowing that none should speak before the Prince did. He sighed "Well! What brings you before me to waste my time!" She bristled. "I came to speak to Princess Myrian. She ordered for me to be brought here."

The prince leaned forward, looking her up and down as if appraising her as a meal. "*Did* she now?" Julia swallowed hard realizing that she hadn't spoken to him using his title. She bowed again "Yes, your majesty" she rose, seeing him gesture to one of his guards. "Take her away. Lady Myrian has no access to letters nor the jurisdiction to send them. This woman is a fraud."

Julia wanted to spit out that he was the fraud! Sitting up there like he owned the world! The guard gently took her by the arm and escorted her out. Out of fear, Julia cooperated but she would get to the bottom of this.

When the guard had taken her out of the throne room he shoved her down a hallway. Fear rose in her throat. She was alone and could very well be used in whatever way this guard thought useful and no one would be able to stop him. "Please! Just let me go there's been some mistake!" she said loudly, trying to draw attention to herself so that she may be able to stop the man from going after her. He quickly put a hand to her mouth pushing her against the wall "Quiet!" he hissed "Lady Myra did send for you, but it was under secrecy of Lord Tico. She is imprisoned, which is why she asked for your help. You are Julia of Fairen correct?" She nodded, wanting to scream in fear. "Good.

Now, I'm going to release my hand from you, and you have to promise not to scream. I will not hurt you, but I must warn you that there are others who will if they get their hands on you. I'll take you to the dungeons so you may see Myra yourself and confirm that you know her. We'll then need a proper statement from you in front of the council. That will be later." He released his hand and stepped back. She stayed tight against the wall, fear still threatened to tighten her throat into a scream, but the man simply held out his hand "This way, Miss." he said politely.

She followed him through passageways, so they only encountered servants as they went. Then they came to a large pair of heavy wooden doors. Four guards stood outside the entrance, armed to the teeth and with harsh looks about them. Julia prayed that she could trust this man. He said "It's Jordan. Let me through." The guards looked at him more closely then opened the doors, inside was a dark stone staircase leading down. Torches flared on the walls, spilling light onto the stairs in weird shadows.
Their footsteps echoed down the stairwell and Julia could feel panic rising. If this wasn't where Myra now resided, Julia would be dead. She'd never be found again. Even if Farrell came looking for her there was no way that he would be able to get her out of this place alive.
She swallowed; trying to remember to breathe.
The room consisted of a line of cells, each not much bigger than a horse-stall. Most were empty and their gates open. But on the end an elderly woman sat inside. Her face was obscured by a tangle of matted hair. Her head rose as Julia entered. "Is this she?" the woman said, excitement in her voice. The guard must have nodded for the woman rose quickly and grasped the bars tightly. "Julia! Oh Julia! I've found you again! I didn't think my letter would find you." The joy bubbled from the woman in waves. Julia couldn't help but smile back at the woman.
"You must be Princess Myrian-" Julia realized her error and quickly bowed. "Your majesty. I didn't mean to offend." She

scrambled. The woman merely laughed "Oh, dear one. You never need bow to me. I have been a commoner too long to ever get used to someone bowing to me. Please stand and just call me Myra."

Julia rose, her eyes flitting from that of the guard behind her and the woman in the cell.

"Please do be comfortable. We wish you no harm." The guard said and quickly found Julia a chair.

"I will be at the stairs. I'm sure you have much catching up to do." He said a quiet smile lighting up his features.

Julia sat- more like perched- on the chair.

"Do I look at all familiar to you, Julia?" Myra asked quietly.

Julia studied the old woman's face. It was full of wrinkles and her hair was in the fashion of the Southlands medicine woman, dreaded with beads and talismans threaded into it. It looked beautiful on the old woman before her. She could see the woman's hands were tattooed with ancient markings.

"I'm afraid, I only have very vague memories of you... I don't remember you having tattoos nor was your hair dreaded in the way of the southland healers. Though I do remember someone with dreaded hair"

Myra nodded, "You are right. It was long before I recognized myself as a healer woman. That may have been Yadira, whom we stayed with for nearly a year. She taught us herbs were for healing and how to use them. These boots she made for me." She stuck out her boot to reveal a worn pair of leather boots, lined with animal skin. "She helped us make parkas too though you may not remember. It was just before you went to the village."

Julia frowned. She couldn't remember any of this. Why wasn't it coming back to her?

"Myra... How old was I when I knew you and why did I go to the village?"

"You were probably 4 or so... I'm not sure why you went to the village." She shrugged "It was where you wanted to go. You hated hunting and didn't like moving around like we did with the pack so I thought it would be a good choice for you."

Julia nodded, pondering the answer.

Willow entered the warehouse, her fiddle case strapped across her back like a shield.
"I'm back" she called out, her voice sending a startled pigeon into the rafters.
"Took you long enough" a voice harrumphed. Willow laughed.
"Well, did you find anything interesting today?" she said unslinging the fiddle and placing in its hiding place behind an old wagon. That was one great thing about this place, it had been a carriage repair house, so the place was well insulated from the cold. Making it a perfect place to keep a weather-sensitive fiddle tucked safely away from thieves and prying eyes.
"Well, if receiving a letter addressed to you from the long dead Pincess of Gandalon isn't interesting I can't imagine what is." Hannah said casually as she came out from behind a wagon, placing an envelope in Willow's hand.
Willow stared at it. The markings looked neat and flowing, as if written by a practiced hand... A well-educated hand.
Willow handed the envelope back to Hannah, her face growing red. "I can't read." she murmured to Hannah's confused expression.
Hannah quickly tried to ease Willow's embarrassment. "Well good thing you have a trustworthy friend to read any secret love letters or other important messages, such as this one!" she said brightly, ripping open the seal and pulling out the letter.

"Addressed to the esteemed Willow the Bard, fiddle player of at The Wild Goose
From Princess Myrianna, fifth daughter of Lord Belloc, the Late king of Gandalon.
Dear Willow, I am in need of your esteemed fiddle playing at a feast I am hosting this evening. Please meet George Fairweather, a personal member of my guard around the back of the palace. I want to keep this a surprise from my lovely nephew Lord Tico. It's his birthday this week! Yours truly,"
Hannah paused, staring a while at the page in astonishment. Looking up at Willow she said slowly, "Marian..."

Willow's head shot up *"Marian!? Our* Marian?"
"I assume so... I doubt a princess would know that you played at a small inn like The Wild Goose and I doubt she would sign it with her everyday common name!"
Willow started pacing. "But *Myra...* a *princess*?! But, the Queen's sister was sacrificed over thirty years ago! Are you sure it isn't a trap?"
Hannah stopped her, holding her shoulders, "It doesn't matter, Willow! You go and you see what this Princess really wants of you! She clearly doesn't want the Prince to know so, it must be something to do with the rebellion! Or, she's in trouble... Might be a trap... But who knows! You've got to go and see!"
"But-I" Willow scrambled.
"You're going there's no buts about it!" Hannah said practically shoving Willow to the changing divider. She threw Willow some dresses.
"Don't just stand there gaping like a fish. Get dressed! You're going to be late!"

Myrianna

Willow and Julia stood in front of Myra's cell, both looking very out of place, dressed to their finest. Willow was dressed in her finest bard clothes, her hair tucked discreetly under a flamboyant hat. Julia was dressed in a fine blue dress that complemented her long blonde hair that flowed down her back.

"Ready?" Myra said excitedly leaning against the bars. A kind of girlish excitement showed plainly on her face and it was that that brought grins to both Willow and Julia's faces. Hannah stood a little way off, dressed in her usual barmaid look. They had agreed that Hannah would better show her authenticity by dressing as herself rather than trying to pretty herself up. Hannah was more than relieved.

Willow grinned openly back at Myra "Ready as I'll ever be! It's your head that will take the axe if we aren't convincing enough." She teased but it made the room grow suddenly somber.

A long silence drew out and Willow kicked herself for being so foolish. Then Myra laughed. A deep hearted belly laugh that made her almost double over.

Soon they were all laughing. The stakes were too high for them to stay serious. They needed to break the tension around their next few moments.

Soon George came down, walking between Willow and Julia. He grabbed the keys and stood in front of Myra's cell. Looking up at her in concern, he asked quietly, "Ready?" Myra's face was serious, the pains of her life etched deeply into her face like old wood splitting from continued wear and tear.

"Ready as I'll ever be" she murmured as they led the way up the stairs with Julia, Willow and Hannah trailing behind.

Inside the large council room sat a heavy oak table, adorned around it were the noble council, decked out in lavish finery. All pompous looking men with arrogance drawn into their every movement, Julia immediately disliked them.
Myra leaned close to her. "If I don't make it out of here alive, know that my life feels complete now that I have reconnected with you. I had always wished to find you again, but I had given up on that dream so long ago... But you're here!"
When Julia smiled and gave her a nod of acknowledgement, Myra's face broke out into a barely suppressed grin.
Myra strode in ahead of George, her chin raised, back straight, and her gait self-assured. Prince Tico sat at the head of the table. When he saw her, he nodded slightly. She curtsied elegantly and sat at the chair George motioned for her to sit at.
"Lord Tico" she said quietly.
"Lady Myra" Tico grumbled.
The others stood awkwardly at the entrance before George escorted them to present themselves to the Prince. Willow bowed low, suppressing a grimace of disgust at seeing his face. The others curtsied and Hannah tapped her slightly with her toe. A reminder to keep her face and emotions in check.

Micareon, Head Councilor stood. "We are gathered here today to judge the integrity of this woman's claim as Princess Myrianna, sister to our late Queen Liana." Julia glanced over to Myra and saw her looking at her toes, whipping away a stray tear that leaked from her cheek. That was what truly solidified the memories as true in Julia's mind. She remembered how authentic and kind and caring Myra had been. This woman who sat before her had only grown in those traits and Julia knew that not a single tear could or would ever be faked by this woman. Julia stood straighter from this realization.

"Let us hear what the witnesses have to say before Lady Myra speaks. I hope that their stories stay untouched by Myra's influ-

ence." Prince Tico drawled.
Willow came forward first, bowing deeply again, keeping a hold on her hat. "My lord, if I may begin my story first?"
The prince stared at her. "State your name, occupation and your connection to Lady Myra"
Willow took a long shuddering breath; Hannah could see that she was like a rabbit, ready to bolt.
"I am Willow, bard of Belloc, especially known at The Wild Goose Inn. I knew Myra... Pardon, Lady Myra as-as" Willow struggled realizing the only connection, she had to the woman was the riots, something she didn't particularly wish the prince to know. "As a storyteller. I first met her when she told me her life story, particularly about her life after being sacrificed to Lord Weirion."
The prince nodded, seeming distracted by something she said. "Next." He said.
Hannah stepped forward next. "My name's Hannah Bradfellow, I'm a barmaid at The Wild Goose Inn and also part of Myra's story, but, what I came here to tell is against the potential evidence of Lady Myra, surrounding Queen Liana's death."
The prince raised an eyebrow but said still nonchalantly "next"
Julia stepped forward, curtsying. "My lord" she said through her bow. "My name is Julia Pinsworth, I am a farmer's wife, living in Fairen. I knew Myra when she lived in the forbidden wood. She saved me from the woods and showed me how to survive. I owe my life to her."
The prince shifted in his seat. "Myra what is your case to prove that you truly are Princess Myrianna?"
Myra sighed, still looking down at her feet. She spoke quietly, forcing everyone to lean in so that they could hear her. Willow suppressed a grin, it was an old trick to get people to really listen to what you had to say. She spoke slowly, as if conjuring up an image from a far-off place.
"Do you remember Tico, how you used to play with the squirrel in the courtyard? You and Suzanne named it Piccalo - after an old story your nursemaid used to tell you. Do you remember

your Aunt Gwen's fabulous stories about Princesses gathering the dragons and fighting an evil king after he tried to slay the dragon and steal her away?" Her voice slowly grew louder. "I was sacrificed in those woods at sixteen. I was tricked by my father, Lord Belloc, into thinking that I would always have a place at the court. That I would always have a home... that I would always belong. Then he abandoned me in those woods, leaving me with my dog, Layrn, who was only a puppy. It was almost winter then. I am Princess Myrian Martenlander because you may recall that I would not do something that was unjust. I never hit you though you were a spoiled prat much of the time I was at court and I see now that you aren't much better." She raised her chin, a sneer of disgust crossing her face. Micareon waved the comment. "Continue, and please stay to the question at hand."

She did not apologize, nor did her eyes stray from the eyes of Prince Tico.

"When you were two, you got a scar on your left foot after playing with a knife your father had given you and accidentally dropping it. You still have that scar, I presume?"

Prince Tico shifted uncomfortably. "Yes" he said quietly, finally having to admit that she was speaking the truth.

Micareon stood again, seeming to try to clear the tension by getting straight to the point.

"Now, we'll have Julia testify to her memory of Myra. When Julia finishes, Myra and anyone else can confirm or deny this story. Let's keep this rolling smoothly shall we?"

Julia sat up straighter. "I was abandoned in the woods at around five or six years of age. These memories are quite hazy for me but based on what my surrogate mother told me, she took me in at about five years of age. She remembered Myra far more clearly than I. Unfortunately, she died last spring, so she can't be here to testify. My memory will have to do."

She took a deep breath; she could see her fingers shaking in nervousness.

"Myra lived with wolves in the forbidden woods. They helped her survive and I met many of them while I lived with her for close to a year. Her dog, Layrn, was one of the kindest dogs I ever met and kept me out of trouble. I remember him and the wolves a little better than Myra I'm afraid. I guess their presence really stood out for me. When Myra found me, I was injured and hungry. I was terrified, but Myra took me in, she helped me learn to survive and thrive in those woods. I didn't realize it at the time but what she taught me and our time together has made me a better person today. I wouldn't have survived without her."

Micareon turned to Myra "Is this true?"

Myra nodded, blinking back tears. She smiled at Julia. Julia smiled back.

"Willow, let's hear your story first."

Willow cursed in her mind. She was trapped. If she'd had more than an hour to decide whether she would even come, she might have been able to make up a decent lie. Now she would be forced to say the truth and risk being killed for it or lie terribly and make Myra's testimony even more shaky.

She swallowed.

"Myra came into the bar one night. She spoke to Marylin at the front. She was kind of strange looking and out of place so I watched her. She looked like a nervous dog, ready to either strike or run at the slightest sound. Marylin, of course, was dying to hear her story, so Myra began and she got so upset that she drew the attention of the entire Inn."

"How was she upset?" the Prince interjected.

"She was yelling. She was angry that no one cared about the sacrificed children and let them die slow and painful deaths. She quickly realized that she had caused a ruckus and immediately excused herself and walked out. Curious, I followed her and asked her to tell me her story.

She did. She spent thirty years in that forest! She saved more than fifty souls and she expected that only ten or fifteen actually survived when they tried to make it out of the forest.

She spent most of her life alone, fending off the wilderness and trying desperately to save the others that were sacrificed. May I also add that she never once tried to start a rebellion. She had perfect opportunity, so many children that were angry and hurt by what had been done to them would have been more than willing to destroy Gandalon. But she didn't. I might also add that the recent riots that led to the law change and Queen Liana's unfortunate death were not started by her. She told me that she wanted the law to change but almost directly after she returned to the woods. I know these streets better than most and I never saw her again, until a few weeks ago, just after she had heard word of Queen Liana's death. She was devastated, it crushed her to pieces. If you don't believe me, then you clearly wouldn't be able to recognize your own mother if she stood in front of you." Willow sat again; her words spent.

Micareon and the others looked at each other a moment.

"Thank you, Bard-Willow for your deep insight." Micareon said, "Miss Fairweather, if you could" he looked at her expectantly.

Hannah stayed sitting for a while, seeming to fight an inner battle of wills. Willow felt bad to put her in this position, but it meant the difference between being ruled by that monster or Myra who had always been honest to her word.

Hannah stood; her tall figure rose over them in an intimidating fashion. Some of the council members straightened, looking worried by Hannah's imposing form.

"I, Hannah Fairweather, swear on my life that what I am about to say is the truth, even though it may kill me in speaking it." She announced, making the council glance at each other in confusion and a slight hint of fear.

"I was there the day Queen Liana died. I can assure you that I never once saw or heard a breath of a whisper that Lady Myra was there. Not under any alias or disguise. I later confirmed that the guards did not see her enter the city until after the Queen was shot. What I did see was His Majesty, Prince Tico on the balustrade of the palace. He was cloaked but I'd have recognized his face anywhere. He was in a corner of the balustrade where he wasn't entirely visible to the guards. I guess he assumed that none of the peasants below him would have the imagination to look around at the decorative railing of the palace walls and spot him whilst the Queen spoke. He had a long bow trained on the Queen. I realized what was going to happen and I went after him, I needed to stop him before he hurt our Queen. Willow unknowingly slowed my reaching him by demanding where I was going. I had gotten to the wall and was trying to attract the attention of a guard, soldier, someone, anyone! But I was too late, Prince Tico saw me and shot the Queen before I had a chance to warn her. I panicked. I thought someone might think I went after her so I took Willow back with me to our place and hid. I told her nothing in case they came after me."

Willow shifted taller in her seat. "I can confirm that I too did not see Lady Myra the day the Queen was killed. I can confirm that Hannah did go into the crowd when the Queen started her speech but I did not know what she was about. She did not have any weapons on her nor did she have any motive to go after the Queen. After all, what we wanted was for the law to change and she did that. We had no reason to go after her."

Micareon nodded and Hannah sat.

"Prince Tico, if the council might have a moment in private to discuss the findings, we'll return and explain our ruling." Micareon said, bowing to the Prince slightly. Prince Tico waved them away and they stepped outside the room, silent until the door shut.

Tico's face grew into a sneer. "How dare you accuse your soon-to-be King of murder! If I have any power, I'll see to it myself that you are hanged for treason of the high court."

Myra straightened; her face hard with anger. "You will not! I can't believe you can sleep at night knowing what you did to Liana! You killed your own mother!"

"She was going to upset the Gods and bring doom upon us all!"

Tico roared.

The door opened loudly, and the council entered.

Everyone sat except Micareon, who stood beside the Prince. He whispered into the Prince's ear, creating an even bigger explosion of aggression from Prince Tico. "WHAT? How can you believe a word that this mad woman says! She's lived the last thirty years in the woods almost completely on her own. She befriended wolves! WOLVES! She's in league with the devil!"

"My lord, Please! These are our findings and you do not yet have power to decide her fate nor that of anyone else in this room. As is the custom with the council we must make a unanimous decision before any actions can be taken outside this room." Micareon towered over the Prince, not so much in size but his actions and voice spoke loud and commanding.

The Prince slammed a fist down on the table, creating an awful whack that made everyone jump.

"She will not take the throne!" Prince Tico said.

Micareon sighed, the sigh encompassing all the hardships that he'd endured as head councilor for the last ten years. "My Lord, I'm afraid that our findings agree that Lady Myra is who she claims and now we will have to sort out this muddled mess around your mother's death." He paused seeming to weigh his words carefully "We heard what you said to Lady Myra and based on the evidence against you, you are under arrest for the murder of Queen Liana. Until we have further evidence to prove the story correct, you will stay as such. George, you may arrest him now."

Tico roared in anger, striking out at the guard, but was quickly caught and held by another guard. They dragged him away, kicking and screaming. The table was deathly silent.

Finally, Micareon addressed them "Lady Myra, as we now have no proof or reasoning to your connection to the murder of Queen Liana and we have confirmed that you are who you claim to be, you are released from imprisonment. Our deepest apologies for ever having doubted you, your Majesty."

Myra's smile slowly grew as if she couldn't believe her ears. "I forgive you, Micareon, for the words you speak now ring most sweetly to my ears." When she looked up at him, her eyes brimmed with tears "Thank you!"

Micareon bowed, smiling too. "You are very welcome your Majesty. I do hope that you will take the Queen's place as leader of our Kingdom."

Myra wiped the tears away with her sleeve, ignoring the fine silk that she was ruining with her tears "It would be my honour."

Queen

Myra sat upon the throne, her long dreaded hair hanging loose behind her, wooden beads clinking within her mane. Her sister's crown rested upon her head, the gold band looking a little out of place with her wild demeanor. She sat at attention on the ornate wooden throne looking every bit like the Queen she now was.

The throne room doors opened, and Myra's breath hitched. Today she would judge the killer of her sister.

Several guards swarmed about Tico. He paid them no-mind as he sauntered up to the throne. A thought struck Myra; Tico would never have known any other way to walk. All his life he had been powerful and had had no knowledge of fear. He stood watching her, a silent battle of wills seeming to cut between them.

A guard cuffed him "Bow to the Queen." Prince Tico raised an eyebrow at the guard, making the guard hesitate. Then Tico bowed in his most arrogant, sarcastic way. His eyes met hers. His pupils blending with the dark brown of his eyes, making him look like a man with no soul.

That would be his punishment. To bring his soul back to himself and show him what he had done, before he would be exiled forever. Myra's eyes grew cold as she stared into the young Prince's eyes.

"Prince Tico, of the Land of Gandalon, you have been accused of murder and treason of the high court and you have been found guilty. You murdered the Queen of Gandalon... Your mother, Liana."

He tilted his head, eyebrows raised in feigned arrogance.

Myra closed her eyes, a deep sigh escaping her lips.

"Your mother... Your mother loved you with every ounce of her being. She wished for nothing more than your happiness and the safety of the kingdom.

She knew that the power of royalty had drugged you and made you forget yourself; the boy who only wished to be loved.

She forgave you, forgave you before she even saw the arrow that killed her. She saw you as you were. A boy who thought he was alone in this world, forsaken whilst those he loved most were held on a pedestal in his mothers' eyes.

Know that you were not abandoned.

She gave me this place on this throne so you might be free to find yourself, to live a life you would never be allowed to live if you were made King. A life of power would have destroyed you, and you may not understand it now, but that life could never be yours.

You are worthy of a life spent helping others, something I have always known that you have been capable of. But your place is not on the throne.

Your place is among the people, something a Queen or King can never hope to experience properly. You have great power within you and a love and passion for life that could move mountains."

Tico's eyes dropped and he slumped against the guards, tears rolling down his nose and onto the floor. Myra swallowed a lump forming in her throat.

"You do not need a chair or a crown to own your power, my boy. That power rests within you. If I have learned anything from my time in the forest, it is that your inner power is all that matters in the end. Everything else is just a title that can be stripped away as easily as the autumn wind strips the leaves off the trees."

When her last words echoed across the hall, the silence soon filled with sobs. Tico kneeled, his head buried in his knees. His body wracked with grief.

"Forgive me. Forgive me mother! I... I never meant... Oh Gods *what have I done*?!" he yelled out into the hall. The guards stood uncomfortably beside him.

Myra stood. "Your mother already forgave you before the thought had blackened your mind. You are forgiven. But we will not forget what you have done. It was the Queen's wish that you are not to be hung. However, you will not walk free.

Therefore... you will be exiled to the forest as I had been.

You will survive, I am sure, but I know that the woods will change you and when you do get called to take the throne when I have passed, you will be a new person. Keep in mind that you will not be protected from arrow or misplaced dagger whilst you live in these woods, that will have to be your responsibility. I am sorry that you will have to take this throne when I have passed. I am too old to produce any heirs, but I will do what is in my power to keep you amongst the woods and the wolves. There you will find the belonging you so desperately crave, and you will make peace with the world."

Myra stepped close to the Prince, the guards grabbed him, pulling him up onto his feet.

"Open your palm" she ordered.

He opened his palm towards her, confusion dancing across his eyes.

Into it she dropped a talisman. A tooth, the root carved into the relief of a wolf.

"I should show you no mercy, but I would not wish your journey on even the lowliest... This is the tooth of Layrn, the dog who was wolf. He saved me more than I ever could save anyone in a lifetime. He was the stone with which I was able to anchor myself when the whole world was lost to me. He was the one who showed me the reason for living.

May he be your guide as he was mine. Keep this on you and the wolves will not bother you. Keep your wits about you and lead always from your heart dear boy.

Tico, your life is not yet lived, take joy that you have many years ahead and remember that power is not yours to wield.
I will do what I can to protect you from the gleaming eye of sovereignty... May the moon guide your journey."
She bowed her head and the guards took Tico away.

Settling heavily upon her throne, she nodded, and her subjects spilled in. From the corner of her eye she saw the flash of a tail and heard the pounding of paws upon the earth, but when she looked nothing was there, only shadows. The memory of a particular howl filled her mind as if she heard it in the room before her. Closing her eyes, she smiled sadly, "Oh, Layrn" she breathed. Then began her place as Queen; healing those who stood before her. The people.

Made in the USA
San Bernardino, CA
26 June 2020